WAYNE STINNETT

Elusive Charity

A Charity Styles Novel

Caribbean Thriller Series
Volume 7

 DOWN ISLAND PRESS

Copyright © 2022
Published by DOWN ISLAND PRESS, LLC, 2022
Beaufort, SC
Copyright © 2022 by Wayne Stinnett
Library of Congress cataloging-in-publication Data
Stinnett, Wayne
Elusive Charity/Wayne Stinnett
p. cm. - (A Charity Styles novel)
ISBN: 978-1-956026-37-5
Cover photograph and graphics by Aurora Publicity
Edited by Marsha Zinberg, The Write Touch
Final Proofreading by Donna Rich
Interior Design by Aurora Publicity
Down Island Press, LLC, a Down Island Publishing company.

This is a work of fiction. Names, characters, and incidents are either the
product of the author's imagination or are used fictitiously. Any
resemblance to actual persons, living or dead, businesses, companies,
events, or locales is entirely coincidental. Many real people are used
fictitiously in this work, with their permission. Most of the locations
herein are also fictional or are used fictitiously. However, the author
takes great pains to depict the location and description of the many
well-known islands, locales, beaches, reefs, bars, and restaurants
throughout the Florida Keys and the Caribbean to the best of his ability.

If you'd like to receive my newsletter, please sign up on my website.

WWW.WAYNESTINNETT.COM.

Once a month, I'll bring you insights into my private life and writing habits, with updates on what I'm working on, special deals I hear about, and new books by other authors that I'm reading.

The Jerry Snyder Caribbean Mystery Series

Wayward Sons

The Charity Styles Caribbean Thriller Series

Merciless Charity	Enduring Charity
Ruthless Charity	Vigilant Charity
Reckless Charity	Lost Charity
Elusive Charity	

The Jesse McDermitt Caribbean Adventure Series

Fallen Out	Rising Force
Fallen Palm	Rising Charity
Fallen Hunter	Rising Water
Fallen Pride	Rising Spirit
Fallen Mangrove	Rising Thunder
Fallen King	Rising Warrior
Fallen Honor	Rising Moon
Fallen Tide	Rising Tide
Fallen Angel	Steady As She Goes
Fallen Hero	All Ahead Full
Rising Storm	Man Overboard
Rising Fury	Cast Off

To our grandson, Jack. Every time you come over, you're a little taller, a little smarter, and more outgoing. I enjoy watching the world unfold through your eyes. Thanks for the inspiration for the characters Jojo and The Buddha.

"It is better to conquer *yourself* than to win a thousand battles. Then the victory is yours. It cannot be taken from you, not by angels or by demons, heaven or hell."
—Buddha

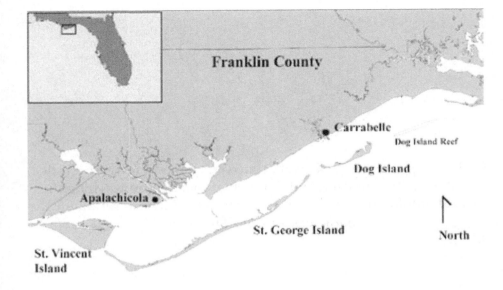

CHAPTER ONE

Saturday, April 23
The Forgotten Coast

The abandoned farmhouse was the perfect location. It was isolated, sitting far down a long dirt track. The property was several hundred acres, backed by a slow-moving river, and the nearest neighbor was a mile on up the desolate county road.

The overgrown track was barely visible from the two-lane highway, as tree branches were growing low over the opening. The mailbox was long gone, and grass and weeds had broken up and hidden the asphalt entry.

It was perfect, Lucas thought, looking around. You could set off a bomb and nobody would bother to come see what happened. There was even a pond with a short dock, so the kids could cool off.

Lucas and two other young men were busy clearing the long dirt drive using rakes, shovels, loppers, and a buck saw. Not exactly the proper tools for the job, but the only ones they could lay their hands on.

The sun was already behind the trees to the west, and it would be dark soon. The track didn't need to be neat and perfect, just clear enough so cars could get through without ending up in one of the ditches on either side.

Lucas looked back at his best friend. "Kenny, what time's everyone coming?"

One of the others stopped what he was doing and glanced over. "Nine o'clock is what was on the invites. We still have an hour or so."

"This was such a cool idea," the youngest of the three said. "There's lots of old places like this all around the county."

Lucas and Kenny had gone to school together since kindergarten but had both dropped out a year earlier, halfway through their junior year at Franklin County School, the only public school in the district. Marc was a year younger—a junior—and still going to school. He was planning to join the Army after graduation the following year.

The abandoned farm was just off Highway 67, nine miles north of the small town of Carrabelle, where the three young men lived. The dismal stretch of two-lane was in the northeast corner of the county, far from any of the small towns along the Forgotten Coast. About a hundred yards behind the farmhouse, the dark waters of the Ochlockonee River flowed southward.

As the three young men got back to work, knocking back the weeds and small trees and bushes that were slowly reclaiming the land, the sound of a car slowing down on the highway beyond the woods caught Lucas's attention. The three looked back down the freshly cleared track and soon a pair of headlights appeared. The three accent lights just inside the headlights gave the car away—a Mustang.

The driver gunned the engine, breaking the Mustang's rear tires loose; it drifted sideways, with the rear tires about to slide into the ditch. The driver eased off and corrected, then slowly rolled towards them.

"It's Leo and Karin," Marc said.

Lucas smiled in the gathering darkness as the car stopped and the window came down.

"Hey, guys!" Leo said. "Great place you have here."

Kenny jammed his shovel into the soft, sandy soil. "Just needed a little sprucin' up," he said. "Have any trouble findin' it?"

"Nah, man. The GPS numbers was a good idea. And the beer cans marking the entrance made it easy."

Kenny had spread the word through social media, giving only a precise position of the entrance and the words "Double Dos." The big twenty-four-ounce green and yellow Dos Equis beer cans with a bright red XX on them would be easily spotted by headlights.

Lucas bent over and smiled at Leo's sister. "How's it goin', Karin?"

She opened the door and got out, looking at the three younger boys over the hood of her brother's car. "Well, I've been here for like ten minutes and nobody's offered me a beer."

"Pull over there toward the pond," Lucas said to Leo. "We have a bonfire all set and two coolers loaded."

"Then let's get this party started!" Leo shouted, dropping the car into gear, and bouncing over the uneven terrain. He spotted the coolers and turned around, so he could back up to the fire pit. Leo always wanted to park where he had a clean exit.

Tossing their tools into the back of Marc's pickup, they followed after Leo on foot, with Lucas and Karin hanging back a little.

"Are you sure your guy's gonna come through?" Lucas asked.

Karin glanced over at him, tossing her long brown hair over her shoulder. "He'll be here," she assured him. "Don't worry about that. Got any weed out here in the weeds?"

Lucas laughed nervously. Karin was almost twenty-one, two

years older than him. He'd had a crush on her since sixth grade, but she'd been an eighth grader and wouldn't have given the time of day to anyone still in elementary grades. She'd dropped out, too, and had taken off with her boyfriend Phil for California, vowing never to return to Apalach.

But here she was, walking right beside him and talking to him. Lucas reached into his shirt pocket and pulled out a pack of cigarettes. He flipped the top and handed her a joint, already rolled, as if it were nothing.

"Cool," Karin said.

She stopped, took it from him, and lit it with her own lighter. When she drew the smoke deep into her lungs, her chest swelled and pointy nipples pushed against the confines of the tank top she wore.

In the glow of the joint, Lucas stared longingly at her breasts for a moment. To say Karin was hot would be an insult. She was small, a little over five feet tall, and Lucas doubted she weighed much over a hundred pounds. Her chestnut-colored hair was wavy and bouncy, but when it was wet, it hung to her bikini bottom.

"Cat got your tongue?" she asked, passing the joint toward him, and blowing the smoke seductively up into the night sky.

"Yeah, um, it looks like it's gonna be a great night."

He puffed on the joint, inhaling the pungent smoke.

She smiled at him in the darkness as he passed the joint back. "That the best compliment you can come up with, Skywalker?"

Though his given name was Luke, the result of parents who were addicted to *Star Wars* movies, he preferred Lucas. Did she know?

"The moon makes you look hotter than ever," he stammered.

She laughed, then hit the joint again. "You're cute, Luke. The moon won't be up for hours."

"Um, well, you still look hot."

She handed the nearly finished joint back. "Keep these coming and I might let you see more."

She turned and trotted toward the others, her hair bouncing loosely. Another pickup came down the long dirt track and parked beside Leo's Mustang.

Lucas got a plastic bottle of lighter fluid from the back of his old Ford pickup, stabbed it with a Buck knife and let the liquid pour over the wood they'd piled up. A match was struck and within seconds, the bonfire was crackling.

Karin hopped up beside Lucas, sitting on the tailgate of his truck.

"Why do you hang around here?" she asked, reaching into his shirt pocket as more cars pulled in.

She opened the pack and took another of Lucas's joints out, holding it up with a questioning look, as the firelight danced across her face, accentuating her high cheekbones, tiny nose, and full lips. Once Lucas produced a lighter and flicked it, Karin puffed a few times, getting it going, then took a long pull, inhaling deeply.

"I've been asking myself that same question since I quit school last year," he replied, accepting the joint from her.

Karin's bare, tanned thigh pressed against his leg, and he could feel the heat through his jeans, wishing now that he'd worn shorts instead. She'd been the prettiest girl in school and now, she was even prettier—an insanely beautiful woman.

"California's great," she said, putting her arms behind her to lean back and stare up into the sky. She began kicking her feet alternately back and forth as Lucas tried to see down her tank top. "Palm trees, clear blue sky, the ocean, and the weather's always perfect."

With each small kick of her left leg, Lucas felt the muscles in her thigh rubbing against him. He could also feel a stirring beginning in his groin.

"Why'd you come back?" he asked, adjusting the bottom of his shirt to hide his hard-on.

"It's also real expensive out there," she replied. "We ran out of money and Phil got arrested."

"How'd you get back?"

"Drove his car and bummed gas money from people in rest stops." She turned her head, as if listening to something. "There it is again."

"What?"

She pointed out behind the house. "Every now and then, I hear water back there."

"It's the Ochlockonee," he said. "It's just across the backyard of the house."

"Come on," she said, jumping off the tailgate. "Show me."

After taking another drag on the joint, Lucas was quick to follow her, and once they were outside the circle of light from the fire, she turned to the right, moving behind the old house, where concrete steps led up to a back door.

"Ever do a shotgun kiss?" she asked, taking the joint back from him.

"What's that?"

"I breathe smoke out while our lips are almost touching, and you inhale." She took a big drag, then motioned him closer.

Lucas, who was several inches taller, had to bend his knees awkwardly to get to her level. She grabbed his head in both hands and put her lips close to his. When she exhaled, he inhaled, drawing most of the smoke into his lungs.

In such close proximity, holding her narrow waist to keep his balance, he was fully excited. It wasn't just the weed that was making him woozy.

"Here," she said, handing the stub of the joint back to him. "You do me now."

"Okay," he said, "but a lot of smoke missed my mouth."

"I'll fix that," she said, stepping up onto the first step of the back porch. "Now we're level."

Lucas drew the hot smoke from the roach in short puffs, inhaling deeply. This time, when he moved his mouth close to hers, she grabbed the back of his neck and head and pressed her lips firmly against his.

Lucas's dark-brown eyes went wide, and he wrapped his arms around her tiny waist, barely remembering to exhale as she inhaled. She practically sucked the air out of him.

One of her legs came up high and locked around his as she pressed herself tightly against him. He put his hands under her butt, and she literally climbed up his body, scissoring both legs around him and locking her ankles together.

She broke away first, dropping to the ground. In the darkness she put a small hand on the front of his jeans and smiled up at him as she rubbed up and down.

"Now that's a shotgun," she said, with a sigh.

Lucas reached for her breasts, but she stopped him.

"Plenty of time for that," she said, taking his hand and leading him back around the corner of the house.

More cars and pickups had arrived. Karin pointed toward a guy standing beside a BMW, apart from the other cars. "That's Antoine. I told you he'd come. Do you have the money?"

"Yeah," Lucas said, a bit dejected. "Five hundred bucks."

"You're gonna clean up," she said, leading him toward the man with the BMW. "Over here, Antoine," she called out.

The man looked toward them and nodded, then moved to the back of his car.

He was small, maybe an inch shorter than Lucas's five-seven, and he was well-dressed. The car was a newer model, probably costing more than any three of the cars parked closer to the fire.

"Did you get it?" she asked, as she and Lucas came around behind the black sedan.

He opened the trunk without a word and produced a plastic jar filled with little white pills.

"How many?" she asked him.

"A hundred hits," he replied. "Just as you asked. Five hundred dollars. Got the money?"

"Pay the man," Karin said, taking the bottle and opening it.

She dumped a few into her palm, looked at them, then looked at the label by the firelight.

Lucas produced a small roll of twenties and handed it to the man. He didn't have to count it—he knew it was the agreed-upon amount.

Antoine, however, did count it. Satisfied, he put it into his shirt pocket and smiled at Karin. "Pleasure doing business with you, *cara.*"

Then the man got in his car and started to back out.

"Cara?" Lucas asked. "Did you give him a fake name?"

Karin smiled and said, "He's Italian. Or at least his folks are. He was born in P'cola. *Cara* is Italian for 'dear.'"

She put the little pill bottle in her shorts pocket, then they returned to the group and sat together on the tailgate of Lucas's truck, the cap's hatch open above their heads. Kenny came over and asked if that had been Karin's delivery guy who'd just left.

"Yes," she replied. "The party favors have arrived."

"Whatcha got?" he asked her.

She leaned against Lucas to dig the bottle out of her tight cutoffs, then held it up. "O.C. Hillbilly heroin."

"How much for five?"

Karin shook five of the oxycodone tablets out of the little bottle and held them out in her hand. "For you, just fifty dollars. But if anyone else asks, it's twenty bucks a pop."

Kenny produced the cash, and she gave him the pills. After he'd gone back over to the fire, she scooted closer to Lucas.

"See?" she said, stuffing the money into his pants pocket and finding him still firm. "Thirty dollars profit, even at the friends and family rate."

More cars arrived. A few people had trouble finding the place and Marc had to walk out to the county road and flag some of them down, but within an hour, there were dozens of vehicles and nearly a hundred young people drinking beer and dancing around the fire to music coming from Leo's Mustang.

The pill bottle was nearly empty and as Karin had promised, Lucas had more than tripled the five hundred he'd started with. She held it up and looked over at him. "Do I get a freebie?"

"Oh, I don't know," Lucas said, starting to feel the buzz from the three beers he'd already had. "Maybe we can work out some sort of a trade."

Karin took one of the pills and seductively moved it to Lucas's mouth. "Are those bean bags back there under the bed cover?"

Lucas let her put the pill into his mouth, then washed it down with the last of his beer. He looked over his shoulder into the darkened recesses of the covered truck bed. The cap had windows, but they were dark tinted.

"Yeah," he replied. "Two big ones."

"Let's kick back and smoke another one with the tailgate all closed up," Karin suggested.

Lucas wasted no time and scrambled backward. When Karin joined him, giggling and squealing, he leaned out and, after a couple of hard tugs, got the tailgate up. Then he reached up and pulled down the cap's hatch and locked it.

Little light from the fire reached the interior, but he could clearly make out Karin sitting on one of the bean bags, her legs stretched out and crossed at the ankles. Her long hair lay sprawled across the yellow bean bag and down over her breasts.

She opened the little container and shook out the last two pills, then twisted her body back and forth seductively, sinking further into the velvet-covered bean bag.

"Two freebies?" she asked, smiling at him.

"That won't be too much, will it?"

"No, I've done two at once a bunch of times." She popped them in her mouth and washed them down with a can of beer.

"Would you take my shoes off for me?" she asked, uncrossing her ankles, and moving one leg over toward where he was still crouched on his hands and knees.

He practically leapt onto the other beanbag and she draped her right leg over his. Reaching down, he lifted her calf, bending her knee so her foot was within reach. Then he did the same with the other foot.

"How long's it take?" Lucas asked.

"Not long." She smiled and moved closer to him. "You'll start to feel it by the time we finish the next joint."

They smoked another about halfway down, their bodies close

together.

"Another shotgun?" Karin asked, her voice a bit slurred.

"Sure," he said, handing her the joint.

She took a deep pull, inhaling and arching her back. Then she motioned for him to come over to her. When Lucas rolled over, propping himself with his hands on either side of her head, she spread her legs and pulled him down on top of her.

Their lips met and she slowly exhaled, pushing her hips up toward him. They soon forgot all about the joint and the party, which was by then in full swing. They kissed and pawed at each other's clothes in a clumsy effort to each undress the other, both laughing as they hurriedly managed to accomplish the task.

She got on top of him first, moving slowly and moaning softly.

Finally, as he felt he was nearing the edge, he rolled her onto the other beanbag, thrusting harder and harder. She moaned in the darkness, and he could see her eyes roll back. Her body fell limp as he moved faster and faster, finally arching his back as he finished.

Exhausted, sweating, and breathing hard, Lucas flopped over onto the other beanbag, spent. When he looked over, Karin's eyes were fixed on the roof of the cap. She, too, looked totally wiped out.

"Karin?" Lucas asked tentatively. "I hope I didn't finish too fast."

She didn't reply. At first, he thought she was just pretending, so he reached over and cupped one of her breasts and squeezed the nipple between his fingers. She'd squealed with delight when he'd pinched her that way earlier. But he got no response this time.

"Karin?" he said, a bit more urgently. "Are you okay?"

Not getting a reply, he moved his hand lower, feeling for her chest to rise and fall as she breathed. Finally, he rolled over and put his ear to her chest.

Silence.

CHAPTER TWO

Sunday, May 1
St. George Island, Florida

The sun was drifting toward the western horizon as a little blue sports car raced southbound onto a long causeway, far exceeding the posted speed limit.

The bridge was over four miles long, mostly raised ten feet above the water on concrete pillars. But it soared higher over the Intracoastal Waterway near the southern end.

The sports car, a Fiat 124 Spider, was the only vehicle on the bridge. The driver stepped on the pedal and after a moment of turbo lag, the little car accelerated even faster.

The bridge was only two lanes, but it had been built much wider than just its travel lanes. There were narrow breakdown lanes between the outer fog lines and the concrete barriers on either side.

Rush hour commuters, what few there were even during the busiest hours, were already sitting at their dinner tables this late on a Sunday. Or maybe they were lounging at their pools with drinks during the last hour before sunset—the Golden Hour. As the sun dropped lower in the clear blue sky, its rays filtered through more and more of the atmosphere, giving everything a rich, warm glow that made colors appear more vibrant.

Many of the homes on the barrier island were vacation rentals, but it was still a while before summer vacationers would arrive and most of the winter snowbirds had left. So, the road was empty.

The top was down on the Fiat. The woman behind the wheel wore large sunglasses, her blond hair streaming back over the headrest. The car approached the hump where the bridge rose sixty-five feet over the ICW and the speedometer showed that the low-slung two-seater was traveling at nearly one hundred miles per hour. Fast, but not the little roadster's top speed, by any means.

Half a mile ahead, another car topped the high span coming in the opposite direction. Though she recognized the grill instantly as a Jeep Cherokee, she lifted her foot anyway and started to slow.

No sense blowing a local off the road, the woman behind the wheel thought.

She started up the incline at just under eighty. As she and the SUV streaked past one another, she saw a flash of blue light on the dash.

"Dammit!" she exclaimed, pounding the palm of her right hand on the gear shift.

In the mirror, she saw the brake lights come on and the Cherokee did a three-point turn at the bottom of the arched part of the bridge, unhindered by any traffic. Then it disappeared from view as the roadster went over the hump and headed downhill.

Highway 303, locally referred to as Franklin Boulevard, was the only way on or off the barrier island, so there was no other option for her but to pull over. Sure, the little sports car could outrun the SUV, but with no place to go, it was pointless.

The Spider continued down the high span as the Jeep with the flashing blue light topped the hump and closed the gap. At the foot of the bridge was a small beach access with a couple of park benches. The blonde downshifted and turned into the small park.

She angled her car to the left, exposing the driver's side, knowing the cop would likely be pretty pissed that she was driving that fast, and she didn't want to cause him any more angst when approaching an unknown car. She remembered being that cop, angry at the carelessness of people, but having to remain calm and careful when approaching a stopped motorist.

"It's just a sunset," Charity Styles said quietly to herself, as she got her driver's license, registration, and insurance card from her purse.

When she looked back over her shoulder, she saw the Cherokee pull in behind her and to her left, angled so as to provide maximum protection for the officer, but out of her own field of view in the mirrors.

She put both hands on the wheel, holding her documents in her left, ready to hand them over. The license was a forgery, but even someone at Florida's Department of Motor Vehicles wouldn't be able to tell. And the phony driver's license number was actually registered through that agency, though she'd never been to a DMV office. All thanks to a friend in Key Largo.

Charity heard the Cherokee's door squeak and then the crunch of shoes on the shell parking area. She blew an errant hair off her cheek.

"License, registration, and proof of insur..." a woman's voice began.

She stopped as Charity extended her left hand. "I'm sorry, Officer," she said, turning to see a dark-haired woman about her own age, standing slightly behind her door, one hand on the grip of the service weapon on her hip. It didn't escape her attention that the holster was unbuckled, the flap tucked neatly behind her belt.

Charity took all that in and more, at first glance. Her dark blue windbreaker was open, the right side pulled back and probably tucked into her pants.

A textbook law enforcement approach.

She was dressed in regular clothes—pleated gray slacks and a white blouse, but the lightweight windbreaker she wore had the Franklin County Sheriff's Office star emblazoned on its left side. It didn't quite go with her outfit.

"Do you know how fast you were going?" the officer asked.

"Yes, I'm afraid I do," Charity replied, wondering if the cop knew.

A Jeep Cherokee wasn't exactly department issue, even in a small rural town like Apalachicola, where having four-wheel drive might be an asset to a deputy, and she wasn't dressed as a patrol deputy, either. A detective using her own car?

If so, the SUV might not even be equipped with radar. She'd seen the Jeep around town, as well as the woman who now stood beside her car. But she didn't know the woman was a cop.

"I've seen you around," the woman said, looking down at the driver's license in her hand. "You're from Homestead?"

"Sort of," Charity replied. "Right now, I'm staying on my boat, anchored northeast of SGI Airport."

"Would you mind stepping out of the car, Ms. Styles?"

The driver's door on the low-slung car opened and Charity slowly unfolded herself from it. She stood and faced the officer, who was quite a few inches shorter. The low angle of the sun made Charity's shadow, stretching across the ground to the cop's left, impossibly long.

The dark-haired policewoman was attractive but didn't flaunt it.

She wore minimal makeup and had her curly, dark hair pulled back in a short ponytail.

"Again, I'm sorry for speeding," Charity offered. "I have no excuse, except I wanted to get back to my boat before dark. I only sped on this long stretch because there wasn't any traffic."

The woman glanced over her right shoulder to the long, empty bridge. No cars had passed since they'd pulled in. Then she looked down at the license in her hand again. "It's still an hour before dark."

"Yes," Charity admitted. "I like to watch the sun go down, and I have a trunk full of groceries to get out to my boat."

"Why are you in Franklin County?" the woman asked

It seemed an odd way to phrase the question—not suspicious, but more akin to disbelief. But Charity had a prepared lie for whenever anyone tried to get too close. She'd used it a couple of times when men in the small town wanted to get to know her better. Most guys didn't want to deal with drama.

"I went through a nasty breakup recently," Charity sort of lied. "This seemed like as good a place to hide as any."

"You're hiding from an ex?"

Charity could see that it was a somewhat touchy subject for the woman. "It's pretty remote here," she said. "He'd most likely look for me in Miami, Palm Beach, or maybe Key West, thinking I'd want to be near what he thought I liked—the big city nightlife."

"Like I said," the woman replied, handing Charity's documents back to her. "I've seen you around town, but not very often. The car kind of sticks out. We're not known for big nightlife here."

Charity took her things back, relieved that she wasn't going to get a ticket but also wondering why. "I'm not into that," she said, looking down at the ground. "Big city or small town. I mostly just stay on my boat, rising and falling with the sun and moon."

"You were in the Olympics."

Charity looked up, surprised, then smiled. "Yes, I was. The 2000 Sydney games."

"A friend mentioned you were in town," the cop said, smiling. "I remember watching you swim."

Thanks," Charity said, always feeling awkward when people remembered her from that part of her life.

"Welcome to Apalach. Try to slow it down, okay?"

"Thanks again, Officer. I will."

"Lieutenant," the cop corrected her. "Lieutenant Margaret Hamilton. But my friends call me Maggie."

CHAPTER THREE

After the Jeep backed in an arc, then took off in the direction it'd been going, Charity started the roadster's engine, and the little turbocharged four-cylinder idled quietly as she watched the Jeep disappear over the hump on the bridge.

She put the shifter in reverse and made the same backing maneuver Lieutenant Hamilton had. The synchromesh reverse gear in the little car's manual transmission whined as she backed up, then shifted to first gear and pulled back up to the road.

Charity turned right, heading into the quiet seaside village. Ahead, Cape St. George Light rose up over the palms and houses. The original lighthouse had been built in 1833 and in 2007, parts of the original one had been used to build the new lighthouse that now stood near the southern tip of the cape.

Charity downshifted as she approached Gulf Beach Drive and turned right. She shifted smoothly up through the gears, but with a residential speed limit of just twenty-five, the lively little car never got above fourth gear. After a half mile, the houses thinned out and Charity accelerated slightly, getting the car into sixth, where it barely loped along at forty miles per hour.

Charity felt bad about having lied to the lieutenant, for both her reason for being in Franklin County *and* her reason for driving so fast.

The truth was that the little Fiat was a thrill and a half to drive.

She'd chosen the area last summer on a whim. The Cayman Islands and South Florida were out, especially the Keys. She'd dissolved her relationship with her former employer in her own way—jetting quickly back to the Caymans to get her boat, then disappearing. There'd been zero chance that she would have gone all the way up to New York to be "debriefed" by Travis Stockwell, Jack Armstrong, or anyone else.

After another mile, she downshifted and turned onto East Sawyer Street, lined with million-dollar-plus homes. When it curved to the left to become North Sawyer, she pulled into the driveway of her friends' house, parking far to the left.

Rudy and Heather weren't at home—it was a vacation getaway—but Charity always left access to the garage in case they came home unannounced.

She'd met the couple soon after arriving in the area last fall. She'd taken a slip at Battery Park Marina because it was outside the forty-four-foot high John Gorrie Memorial Bridge. Her mast height, with the gaff-rigged mainsail lowered, was just a foot shy of that, so staying at one of the other marinas would have meant arriving or leaving at low tide, so she wouldn't knock her antennas and cameras off the top of the mast.

The couple kept a boat at the same marina, docked directly astern of Charity's boat, *Wind Dancer*, and while visiting one weekend, they'd introduced themselves. They'd first started talking about sailing, which led to where each had been, which turned out to be a lot of ports and anchorages in common. Rudy and Heather Haverstock were easy people to like.

After walking around the side of the house, both hands loaded with canvas tote bags, Charity started out onto the long dock. When she reached the end, she set her bags near the edge and climbed down into her rigid-hull inflatable dinghy, or RHIB, and started the engine. While it warmed up, she loaded her groceries into the front of the little boat, then untied the line. In seconds, she was zipping across the water toward *Wind Dancer.*

She slowed as she approached, marveling at her boat's long, elegant lines silhouetted against the setting sun. She'd been built ninety years earlier, long before fiberglass and electronics. But *Wind Dancer* was the proverbial wolf in sheep's clothing. Not that she'd win any races against much lighter fiberglass boats of an equivalent size, but she could boast the latest in advanced electronics and sail-planning software that could actually control the boat. Not just an autopilot, but computer software controlling electric winches for trimming the sails.

And *Dancer* could more than hold her own in heavy seas. As her friend Jesse McDermitt often said, "Slow is smooth and smooth is fast." When other boats had to take shelter or heave to, *Dancer* needed only to minimize sails and press on. She had a full lead keel and six-and-a-half feet of draft. A true blue water passage-maker and had crossed oceans.

Charity pulled up alongside the much higher sloop and tied the painter off to the mid-ship cleat, letting the dinghy drift back to the boarding ladder.

She pulled a small handgun from a holster under her shirt and climbed quickly to the deck, the Diamondback DB9 held low against her thigh.

There was no place on the deck for a person to hide, except on the far side of the cabin top, but even there, they'd have to lie flat on the far side deck, as the cabin rose only slightly more than a foot above them.

She mounted the cabin top, ducked under the boom with the hammock suspended below it, and satisfied herself there wasn't anyone hiding above deck.

Stepping down into the cockpit, she approached the companionway hatch and checked the little double doors. The hair she'd plucked from her head before leaving was still there.

Holstering the compact 9mm semi-automatic, she unlocked the hatch, slid the top forward, and opened the two swinging doors below it before retrieving her bags.

Looking back over her right shoulder, she saw the sun was still fifteen or twenty minutes above the horizon and the high span of the bridge was the only part visible. She had plenty of time. She carried her bags down into the salon, placing them on the countertop before going forward to her stateroom.

Charity opened the large deck hatch above her bed and a cooling breeze entered, flushing the heated air back through the boat and out the companionway hatch. She stashed her pistol under the pillow, then undressed, tossing her blouse and shorts into a laundry basket before going aft wearing just the bottom part of a bikini. Though technically it was barely spring, it'd been hot and muggy all day.

She quickly put the groceries away, got a bottle of water from the small refrigerator, and headed back up to the cockpit. Dinner could wait. Charity had a date with the hammock.

Stretching her long legs out, she relaxed and watched as the sun began its evening ritual. She sipped from the water bottle and thought about the events that had brought her to the Forgotten Coast.

Would I do it again if given the chance? she asked herself.

She knew the answer. She would. But she might make the torment last longer. The man she'd killed in San Juan Harbor, aboard *Heart and Soul*, had needed killing. He'd been lucky she hadn't disemboweled him as he hung, struggling in his bathtub.

Most of the world thought that Joel Eisenstein had accidentally hanged himself while engaged in something called auto-erotic asphyxiation. Only a few knew the truth. And that was why she'd disappeared.

The man was a pedophile who preyed on young girls, luring them into his sick world with more money and power than any one man ought to have. And when he'd finished with them, he killed them. At least one, anyway. Charity felt sure there'd been others, and some had probably met an even worse fate than he did.

But in killing the pervert, she'd severed ties with Armstrong Research. Her closest friends were associated with the company, so she'd cut contact with them, except Chyrel, who'd provided her with the fake driver's license and passport, both in her real name.

She'd told Charity that the information in Florida's DMV database, as well as Customs and Immigration, were bogus and not searchable by name or address. Searching either database by name or address resulted in her real driver's license and passport documents, neither of which had been used in over eight months.

Had Lieutenant Hamilton run her license, she'd likely have used the driver's license number; common procedure when Charity had been a cop in Miami, since there were literally dozens of people with the same name. Some, like John Smith, could number in the thousands just in one state. Chyrel had told her that a search by either her driver's license or passport number *would* result in the phony documents with the same address and a clean driving record with no wants or warrants. But only if searched by the number. That meant anyone trying to find her by name wouldn't see the phony driver's license number—only her original.

Chyrel had assured her that she could use her own name anywhere she went, which made things much easier. She knew she could trust the woman. She'd once been a computer analyst with the CIA, and spooks could lie to their mother without her seeing it.

The sun got lower, heading toward a spot just to the right of the point of land at St. George Airport. Looking toward the east, sunlight shone on the bridge's high arch where it appeared to rise up out of the water like the back of some kind of serpent before diving back again; only the upper three-fourths of the arch was visible due to the distance.

A splash caught Charity's attention and she looked in the direction from which it'd come. Heather Haverstock was on a paddleboard, just twenty yards away.

Charity stood and stepped down to the side deck, unconcerned about her semi-nudity. Heather's paddle paused for only a second, then she continued closer.

"Hi, Charity," she called out, stopping a few feet away. "Sorry to disturb you."

"Just watching the sunset," Charity said, making no move to cover herself. "I didn't know you were home."

"We heard your dinghy motor when we were unpacking," she said. "We just got here about an hour ago ourselves. By the time Rudy ran down to the pier, you were already in your little boat and couldn't hear him."

Charity looked past her at the house. A single light shined from an upstairs window. "Is something wrong?" she asked.

"No, no," Heather said. "Nothing like that. We just wondered if you'd like to have dinner with us. Rudy's going to fire up the grill in a bit and we picked up some chicken before coming out."

"I just bought groceries in town," Charity replied. Then, noting a frown form on the younger woman's face, added, "But it would be nice to have a visit. Can I bring anything?"

Heather smiled. "No, we have everything. Say in about an hour?"

"I'll be there."

"Great," Heather said. "I look forward to catching up."

Then she expertly turned the board around and started paddling away.

Charity went back to her hammock and lay in it. The sun was halfway below the horizon. As it got smaller and smaller, Charity closed her eyes for a second and made a wish. When she opened them again, the last of the sun winked and disappeared.

She hadn't expected to see the green flash, but she made her wish all the same. The western end of the long, crescent-shaped island was several miles away, on or just over the horizon, and she felt the rare phenomenon was more dependent on the sun setting over deep water.

In the opposite direction, the higher part of the bridge was still bathed in orange light. It also grew smaller and smaller, until the bridge, too, was in the shadow of the horizon—another sunset.

Rising from the hammock again, Charity looked toward the Haverstocks' house. Heather was already at the dock, climbing up with a leash on her ankle. When she reached the top, she pulled the board up and stowed it, then hurried along the dock, her blond locks bouncing as she almost ran.

Charity descended the companionway steps, wondering what

Rudy Haverstock was going to think when his wife told him how Charity had been dressed.

Rudy was a software developer and owned a successful company. All his employees worked remotely, primarily in India, which allowed him to telecommute from anywhere with Internet, cell phone, or satellite access.

Heather owned a thriving graphic design business. She'd told Charity that a lot of her work was in putting together video ads and editing short documentaries and vlogs. She needed only a laptop and occasional Internet access.

The couple traveled extensively, usually by air, working and playing in vacation hotspots all over the world, but they also spent the winter months cruising the Bahamas, Mexico, and the Caribbean aboard their forty-six-foot Hylas.

Modern day jet-setters.

But they weren't obnoxious like many wealthy people Charity had met. She too, was in fact quite wealthy. Which, so far, had made it pretty easy to disappear, even using her own name. She hadn't yet touched any of her bank accounts or offshore numbered accounts. Thanks to the pervert, she had enough cash on her boat to last a hundred lifetimes.

He'd left this world with twenty-five million dollars' worth of Brunei dollars in a briefcase when he'd gone to Charity's cabin to kill Valentina. That had been his last mistake.

They were all B$10,000 notes, worth over $7,000 each in U.S. currency.

Charity had given one of the foreign currency bundles, worth at least $700,000, to Valentina, the young girl she'd befriended on the yacht. Since then, Charity hadn't had to exchange any of the Brunei bills, but her pile of American dollars was getting low, and she would have to find a bank to exchange one or two in the not-too-distant future. Fortunately, banks in harbor towns were used to dealing in foreign currency. Still, she thought it might be better to travel to a larger port city, like Mobile or New Orleans, where exchanging a larger denomination foreign bank note was less likely to raise any eyebrows.

Charity ducked her head and stepped the rest of the way down into the salon, where she checked the water tank gauge. She'd run the generator and water maker the previous day for nearly eight hours, while doing a thorough cleaning of *Dancer's* interior, all the way down to the bilges and tiny engine room.

The eight hours of running time on the little diesel generator used almost two gallons of fuel, but it had been worth it. Her water tanks were nearly full—almost seventy gallons of fresh water.

She stripped off the bottom of her swimsuit, stepped into the small head, and turned on the hot water. When she saw steam, she moved into the stinging spray, letting it fall onto her head and shoulders, and trace undulating rivulets down her body. Then she turned it off, switched over to the raw seawater rinse and lathered up. With a final hot rinse from the small water heater to get the soap and salt off, she stepped out of the head, dripping wet, her skin practically scalded to a dark red.

Wind Dancer's sole was teak, nearly impervious to moisture. The water that dripped from Charity's body as she went forward to her little cabin would dry or make its way into the bilge, then be pumped out.

"Now, what do I wear to a rich couple's house for dinner?" she mused aloud, opening her wardrobe, and perusing her options. Her choice was limited. "Sailing attire, it is."

CHAPTER FOUR

Less than an hour after sunset, Charity got into her dinghy wearing white shorts and an apricot-colored tank top. As she approached the spacious T-head of the Haverstocks' long pier, she couldn't help thinking it was such a waste when they couldn't even bring their boat to their dock.

To reach water deep enough for their awfully expensive Hylas yacht, the dock would have to be extended at least half a mile, almost to where *Wind Dancer* lay at anchor in ten feet of water. The Hylas only drew six-and-a-half, but there was an eight foot ledge a short distance toward shore and if the wind was out of the north, waves on the south side of Apalachicola Bay could bounce her off the bottom at low tide.

She tied up to the dock and stepped out of her dinghy, running her fingers through her normally wavy blond hair to get some of the tangles out. It was quite a bit longer than she usually wore it. Long hair tangled easily in the wind and water. Fortunately, it was still slightly wet from the shower and hung straighter.

Charity turned and started toward the foot of the pier. As she got closer, she could hear soft music of some kind—a resonating, ringing sound that rose and fell like waves on a shoreline.

Rudy and Heather weren't alone. She saw two strangers—one on the deck overlooking the backyard and Apalachicola Bay, and the other sitting in the grass with his back to the water, playing some kind of musical instrument.

As Charity got closer, she saw that the musician was an exceptionally large, very round, older man and the instrument he was playing didn't appear to be a musical instrument at all, but brass bowls of some kind. His hair was shoulder-length, and he wore a full, bushy beard, mostly white. He was dressed in traditional-looking Hindu garb.

The other man stood by the grill with Rudy, the two conversing in low voices. This man was smallish, probably in his forties, clean-shaven, mildly attractive, and seemed fit for his size. He wore pleated khaki pants and a short-sleeved, dark blue shirt. On his feet were well-worn Topsiders, while the heavyset, bearded man was in bare feet.

She took in all these minute details and then some, giving only a cursory glance to the two men and their surroundings. In her mind, she didn't see them as threatening, but she also chose points of cover and egress.

"Ah, Charity," Rudy said, when he saw her approaching. He turned and called through the open sliding glass door, "Heather, Charity's here."

Charity stepped past the man sitting on the grass and strode up onto the deck, as he continued moving wooden mallets around the rims of several bowls, making an almost eerie sound. His eyes were closed.

"Hi, Rudy," Charity said, accepting a quick hug from her friend.

"So good to see you again," Rudy said, sweeping an arm to the man by the grill. "This is our friend Jojo."

The man smiled at her, extending a hand. "When Rudy told me

you were here, I begged him for an introduction."

Like the bearded man, Jojo was dark-skinned, and there was just a trace of some Mediterranean or maybe Southwest Asian accent. Turkish or Indian, maybe.

"You know me?" Charity asked, shaking his hand, but finding it odd to be recognized twice in one day.

"We went to UCLA at the same time, but we never met. I graduated the same year you set the school's one-hundred-meter freestyle record—your sophomore year, I think it was. I followed your career all the way to Sydney, but then you disappeared from the swimming circuit shortly after winning an Olympic bronze medal."

"Nice to meet you," Charity said, just as Heather stepped out through the open door.

"Charity, I'm so glad you could come," Rudy's wife said, placing a large salad bowl on the outdoor table, which was set for five people. She lifted a bottle. "Care for a glass of wine?"

"Maybe later," Charity replied, thinking it best to stay sober.

"Later, then," Heather said, putting the bottle down and giving Charity a hug. "Jojo and The Buddha have been dying to meet you ever since Rudy mentioned your name a few weeks ago. We had no idea you'd been an Olympic athlete."

Charity glanced over at the man playing the bowls. "The Buddha?"

"Jojo and The Buddha are our spiritual advisors," Rudy said. "They flew down a week ago."

"From where?" Charity asked.

"New York," Jojo replied. "The Buddha teaches tantric meditation at a school in Manhattan."

"Is that his real name? *The* Buddha?"

"Of course not," Jojo said with a charming smile. "What kind of parents would name their child that? His name is Daljeet Khatri, and my given name is Jyotiraditya Laghari. But please don't try to pronounce it, I have been Jojo since I was five. That was when my family moved to California from Bangladesh."

Charity glanced back over at the man sitting on the grass again. "Is he...meditating?"

Heather laughed. "Sort of. It's kind of a cross between meditation and performance. The bowls produce a healing sound for anyone who hears them."

The ringing of the bowls continued, slowly fading as The Buddha rose from his cross-legged sitting position and made for the deck.

"Hello," he said, smiling in a way that pulled his cheeks out above his beard. "You must be Charity Styles."

Charity extended a hand. "I am. I love the sounds you were making."

He shook her hand with both of his, then looked back to where he'd been sitting. "Would you like to try it?"

Charity shook her head. "I don't have a musical bone in my body."

"Nonsense," The Buddha said, not letting go of her hand, but leading her out onto the grass. "Sound therapy is a very ancient form of regeneration. All people have songs in their hearts. The bowls bring them out. Sit here."

She felt goofy but sat down anyway—if nothing else, just to appease her friends.

"There are two ways to make the bowls sing," he said, crossing his legs and lowering himself next to her. "You can strike it with the puja, or mallet." He picked up a small wooden mallet with what looked like felt wrapped around the end, and gently tapped one of the medium-sized bowls.

It rang like a bell for several seconds.

"The other way is called rimming," he said, gently rubbing the mallet around the edge of a larger bowl. "Friction and slight imperfections in the mallet cause minute vibrations on the rim, which are transmitted back to the mallet, where it in turn causes more vibration and a rising pitch."

Slowly, the bowl started to ring, the pitch wavering as he moved the mallet around the edge, first at an angle, then more vertically.

"You try," he said, extending the mallet toward her.

She took it and gently struck the biggest bowl. The ring it made was like a train horn, far up a winding valley.

"I like the deeper tones, also," The Buddha said, smiling through his beard. "You have just played a G note, so you do, in fact, have the ability to make music. The G is red and it is the tone for the root chakra. Making that bowl sing will remove blockages and bring balance to the root of your body. Try rubbing the mallet back and forth along the rim, slow and steady—as if you were slicing a bread loaf."

She did, and soon the bowl began to resonate so low she almost couldn't hear it—a deep, thrumming sound.

"A little slower, with a longer stroke," he instructed.

When she did as he said, the bowl began to hum with a heavy bass note that reminded her of the low, guttural sound of the didgeridoo, a large wind instrument of the Australian people.

"Yes," The Buddha said softly. "Continue doing that with your right hand." He picked up a second mallet. "Are you one of those people who can rub your belly and pat your head at the same time?"

"Ambidexterity? Yes, it's practically a requirement for athletes."

He smiled again and Charity sensed the man had a serene, very calming nature. "Good," he said, putting the second mallet in her left hand. "Take this puja and slowly trace circles very lightly around the rim of the blue bowl by your left foot."

The bowl had an image of a large, branching tree on the inside and some sort of writing around the outside. She put the second mallet against it and moved it in full circles, in time with the sawing motion of her right hand. The smaller bowl began to emit the higher, eerie sounds she'd heard from the pier.

"That note is a C," The Buddha said. "The tone for the heart chakra. The two sounds are harmonious, are they not?"

Charity nodded.

"The heart chakra is green, exactly opposite red on a color wheel. Do you know the wheel?"

"Yes," Charity replied softly, enjoying the soothing sounds she was making. "I remember it from art class in grade school."

"You are a musician, Charity Styles."

Charity looked over at The Buddha and smiled. "Two notes doesn't make someone a musician."

"Everyone must start somewhere," he said gently, as Charity continued making the bowls sing. "Close your eyes and let your third eye guide you. Allow your hands to move of their own volition, and just let your mind escape. You may feel as if you are floating."

She closed her eyes and let her hands trace the edges of the bowls by feel, having found a pressure she liked. The sound was soft and very soothing. It seemed as though it came from another world, from everywhere at once and nowhere at all. It was a very ancient and uplifting sound.

Charity found that by varying the pressure of the mallet on the two bowls, she could raise and lower the volume of the sound, and that by changing the angle of contact, she was able to slightly raise and lower the pitch. For a moment, she did feel as if she were floating.

Then the mood disappeared. She opened her eyes and stopped her hands. "That was weird."

The Buddha smiled. "You have been playing for ten minutes."

She looked into his calm brown eyes with disbelief. "How long?"

He nodded slowly. "Ten minutes. As I have heard people in your country say, the worm has turned for you." He picked up the blue bowl. "Take this," he said. "Play it when you feel tense or full of negativity."

"I couldn't accept—"

"Please," he said, extending it to her. "I insist. It will help to heal your heart."

Charity didn't believe he could possibly know what she felt, how she hurt thinking of the past. With the future unwritten, she'd always focused on the now. She'd never talked to Rudy or Heather about her previous life, the loves she'd lost, or the things she'd done. The man had no way of knowing that her heart was wounded and calloused many times over.

"Thank you," she said awkwardly.

Charity had never been good at accepting gifts or help with anything. But The Buddha seemed so genuinely giving, she couldn't possibly not accept the gift. And she did like the sound.

CHAPTER FIVE

Chapter Five

Later that night, after Charity had returned to *Wind Dancer*, she'd felt calm and relaxed. Jojo and The Buddha seemed to bring balance and a serene awareness to their surroundings and to her and her friends.

Usually, when she was with Rudy and Heather, their conversations had been about sailing, or the couple's work. They often tried to coax a little about Charity's past from her.

But over dinner, there was no cruising talk, even though Charity suspected that Jojo was a sailor. Nor was there any discussion about software or graphic art or business or politics. The conversation was light and revolved more around feelings and how people fit into their personal worlds, and how each of their worlds changed as people came and went. Not as husband, wife, friend, businessperson, or employee, but more spiritually.

Charity had been surprised, not just at her friends' interest, but that she had actually been able to contribute, though she couldn't understand why. She'd never been religious.

Charity was a loner. She had very few friends before her involvement with Armstrong, saw them rarely, and stayed connected by the occasional email. More recently, she'd had close ties with a few people at Armstrong, but now that she'd cut ties with the corporation, she was rarely in touch with any of them, except Chyrel. But they'd been as close as family, much like in the Army. While still with them and working in various parts of the world, they'd kept in touch frequently.

Lying in her bunk, enveloped in a cocoon of darkness, she studied the faint outline of the exposed wood frames of her cabin, knowing where every scratch and knot in every board was located without being able to see any detail in the low light.

When she looked up through the open hatch above her head, she could see thousands of stars just in the little eighteen-inch-square opening. Ursa Major, the great bear, was directly above.

She and Victor had lain in her small cabin staring up at the night sky for hours, as, one by one, the stars, planets, and constellations scrolled across the small hatch.

Charity tilted her head slightly, looking into the salon.

The gift from The Buddha lay on the midship counter, under which *Dancer's* engine was located. The hatch above it allowed air and starlight in, illuminating the brass parts of the bowl, which seemed to glow with some internal, ethereal light.

Charity sat up in bed and gazed at the bowl. She'd really enjoyed the few minutes she'd made The Buddha's bowls sing. That's what he'd called them—singing bowls. Each was hammered into shape by hand over a fire. She rose and strode through the salon to the small galley, her eyes fixed on the bowl.

A moment later, she found herself on the foredeck, placing the small bowl on a silk cushion. Naked, she sat cross-legged on the teak deck. She held the mallet in her right hand and gently struck the bowl.

She was unworried that anyone would see her. Nobody was close enough to make out any detail, and it was doubtful anyone was even looking toward her boat. And if anyone were looking and did see her naked, it still wouldn't bother her. She'd shed her inhibitions a long time ago.

Surrounded by darkness, *Wind Dancer* floated tranquilly at anchor half a mile from shore. With no wind or waves lapping at the hull, the ring of the bowl seemed loud. She put her fingers lightly on the rim, stilling it, then picked up the bowl, balancing it on the palm of her left hand, and struck it again, much more lightly.

A slight, cooling breeze tickled her bare flesh as the note rang, and she peered out around her boat. The water was as dark as ink, barely illuminated by the stars overhead. It resembled a black satin sheet, scarcely moving of its own accord. The small spit of land where the Haverstocks' house sat appeared to be farther away than it did during the day. There was a faint glow of light coming from two of the windows on the left—the living room. All along the shoreline, only a few lights were visible in other houses and, far in the distance, Cape St. George Light flashed its warning to mariners.

There was nobody around to see or hear her. She was as alone as a person could be.

Placing the bowl back on the cushion, she lightly touched its edge with the mallet, slowly sawing it back and forth. The bowl began to sing, and she changed her sawing motion to a circular one. She could feel the vibrations throughout her body.

The soft tone was soothing, and she closed her eyes, letting her mind drift as the sound reached deeper into her subconscious. Slowly, a warmth began to emanate from her chest, spreading throughout her body.

Charity's eyes suddenly blinked open.

The sky above was blue, with puffy white clouds drifting slowly on the upper-level winds. She tilted her head and could see water just beyond the boat's toe rail. She was lying on her back on the foredeck.

Slowly, Charity sat up, feeling a little confused—a strange sensation for her. Confusion was seldom in her nature. She often slept in strange places, many times, away from her boat. Her subconscious always knew where she was and how she'd gotten there, and she'd always been instantly aware of those elements upon awakening.

The little bowl sat on the deck beside her. She remembered sitting down what seemed like just a few minutes ago, and making the bowl sing, then closing her eyes.

"Double weird," she said, getting to her feet.

She picked up the bowl, puja, and the little donut shaped cushion, then held the ornate brass piece in her palm, studying the writing on the side. She'd never seen the figures and had no idea what language it was, or if it was even writing at all.

The sun was about an hour above the horizon, telling her that it was around eight o'clock. It'd been just before midnight when she'd returned from dinner at the Haverstocks'. She'd slept soundly on the hard deck for eight hours.

Surprisingly, Charity felt no soreness or stiffness anywhere as she made her way aft to the companionway hatch in the cockpit, only slightly aware that she had nothing on.

After descending the ladder, she carried the bowl, mallet, and cushion to her little stateroom, where she placed them on the shelf opposite her bunk.

She took a deep breath and let it out slowly, realizing she felt better than she had in a long time. And she was hungry. Back in the galley, she peeled and sliced a banana as she put a skillet on the stove to preheat. Next, she grabbed some eggs from the little refrigerator and a small Spanish onion and green pepper from the hanging veggie net. While the skillet heated, she ate the chunks of banana and diced the peppers and onions to add to the omelet.

When she reached for the coffee pot, she stopped herself and opened a bottle of water instead. She was wide awake, alert, and didn't need the stimulation.

Once the omelet was ready, she sat down and ate ravenously, then cleaned the dishes and put them away.

The writing on the side of the bowl intrigued her. She grabbed her cell phone from the charger and took it with her to the stateroom, where she took pictures of the markings. Using Google image search, she tried one, then two of the odd markings together, then the second and third together, then the first three all in one image.

"Breathe in?" she said aloud, reading the results of her search.

She did the same with the next three of the six markings. The result was as she expected.

"Breathe in" and "Breathe out" were inscribed on the bowl in Nepali script.

CHAPTER SIX

The VHF radio crackled in the salon. "*Wind Dancer, Wind Dancer,* this is *Antares.*"

Charity put the bowl back and went aft to the radio mounted under the steps. Taking the mic from its holder, she pressed the button on the side.

"*Antares,* this is *Wind Dancer.* What's up, Mike?"

Mike Rostock owned a fishing charter business on the mainland, not far from where Charity had first docked her boat. His wasn't a big operation, just him and a Mako center console. But with his wife's help, they were doing quite well. She was seven months pregnant with their first child, but she still went out with him most times.

"Got a charter today and Brenda's not feeling well."

"I wouldn't expect so," Charity said into the mic. "Where are you fishing?"

"Offshore," Mike replied. "I could use someone to drive the boat while I work with the anglers."

"You'll have to pick me up, feed me lunch, and bring me home," Charity offered, knowing that Mike would have already asked any other possible crew. Finding someone on short notice couldn't be easy.

"Thanks," he replied. "We'll be there in half an hour."

"Roger that," Charity said. "*Wind Dancer* standing by on seventeen."

Going forward, Charity opened a drawer and put on a red one-piece swimsuit she'd bought in Pensacola, then donned a pair of baggy khaki pants and a white, long-sleeved fishing shirt over the swimsuit.

Knowing Mike would have ample drinking water onboard, she brought only a half finished bottle up to the cockpit, pulling the top hatch closed. She plucked a hair from her head and inserted it between the two lower doors, then locked up the boat.

Waiting in the cockpit, she was sipping her water when a sudden realization hit her. She'd not only slept all night on the hard deck with no discomfort, but she'd awakened not remembering having dreamt.

Dreams came to Charity just about every night, and when she woke, she remembered them, dissected, and inspected them, trying to understand what they meant. Most were benign, but at least once or twice a month, the dreams were incredibly real and horrific.

Far to the north, she could just make out a big center console moving south in the channel that branched off the main one, the ICW, which ran almost east to west through the bay and went straight into Apalachicola.

When the boat passed the upper anchorage in water deep enough it didn't need the channel, it turned out of it and headed straight toward her.

Charity rose and went up the starboard side to the shrouds, where two fenders were secured, then carried them back abeam the cockpit, and secured them to two lifeline stanchions there.

Soon, she recognized *Antares*, Mike's thirty-three-foot Mako center console, and grabbed her big, floppy hat from behind the dodger, waiting while Mike used the joystick controls to turn *Antares* around and smoothly bring her alongside.

Then she held onto Mike's hardtop Bimini and stepped over onto the gunwale and then down onto the deck. *Antares* never even bumped her fenders.

"Thanks for doing this," he said, maneuvering away from *Wind Dancer.* "The clients are just a mile east of here, at a rental house."

"Don't worry about it," Charity said. "Just have Brenda make me one of those mango pies and we'll call it even. Who are your clients?"

Mike pushed the throttles forward, bringing the boat up on plane as he turned slightly right.

"Three guys who come down here every year with their families," Mike replied. "They're okay, I guess. I just don't understand why they always leave their wives and kids while they're here on vacation with them."

He angled northeast, heading toward the ICW. The bay was considered shallow, and it did have some shallow areas. The channels were for heavier boats, big shrimpers with deeper drafts. With five feet of water just about everywhere you could go in the bay, Mike didn't have to worry. At idle, his boat probably drew less than two feet, and maybe half that on plane.

They rode for a minute in silence, the sun shining on both their faces. Charity didn't bother with any questions about how his wife's pregnancy was going. It was something she'd never experienced and couldn't contribute to a discussion on the subject.

"You know Rudy and Heather, right?" she asked, raising her voice slightly to be heard over the twin 350 horsepower outboards.

"Not well," he replied. "Met them a few times, but we're not close or anything."

"Do you know their friends, Jojo and The Buddha?"

He laughed. "Jojo and The *Buddha*? Seriously?"

"I take it you've never heard of them. They're from Bangladesh, or at least Jojo is."

"Never heard of them," Mike replied, slowing the boat and turning back toward the island. "There's our guys."

Mike's clients were law partners from north Georgia. They seemed easygoing as the group headed out for a day of fishing on the Gulf of Mexico. It was obvious they knew Mike quite well and they weren't clumsy on the boat. Mike introduced each of them, and they'd all talked about the previous day's trip. They apparently had Mike booked for four straight days, all day.

For the most part, Charity just drove the boat and the clients seemed to know better than to bug her. Occasionally, Mike joined her at the leaning post to check their location or give her a new destination. He was enjoying himself, in his own element with the fishermen. And he was earning almost enough money with the four-day charter to cover his expenses for the whole month. The young couple was happy, successful, and they hadn't yet reached thirty.

Mike knew the coastal and inland waters intuitively. His dad had been a shrimper, as had his father before him, and Mike had spent every summer out on the water with his father and grandfather since the age of seven.

Throughout the day, the clients caught quite a few fish, keeping only a select few, which Mike cleaned, expertly filleted, and put on ice. By midafternoon, they were headed back toward shore, happy with the day's outing.

Charity steered a course on the chart plotter, straight toward the inlet to St. George Sound at the east end of the island.

She couldn't see shore yet—they were still five miles away—but suddenly several of the men's phones began ringing and vibrating. They'd put them all in a dry tray behind the windshield.

"Uh, Mike," Charity said, getting his attention. "Everyone's phone's ringing like crazy."

"That's normal," Mike replied, stepping under the T-top and checking his own phone. "We're right on the edge of the cell tower's range. Nothing for me."

One of the fishermen, the senior partner of their firm, reached past Mike and picked up his phone. "Back to the land of reality," he said, chuckling at his own joke.

He tapped the screen a couple of times, then his face drained of color. He looked up at Mike, then back at one of the other men, sitting on a fold-down seat with his back to the transom. Then he stared back down at the screen.

"Something wrong?" Mike asked him.

The man, who Charity remembered was called Angelo, looked up at the younger man. "Al's son," he stammered. "He's dead."

CHAPTER SEVEN

With Mike at the helm, they'd raced at top speed back to St. George Island. The boat had become airborne several times, launching off the low-rolling waves, but Mike was in full control, throttling back when the engines' lower units came out of the water to keep them from overrevving, then back to full throttle just as the stern made contact with the water's surface again.

When they arrived at the rental house, there was a crowd of people waiting at the dock—several women and half a dozen kids. Charity recognized only one person: Lieutenant Hamilton stood off to one side of the dock wearing the blue Franklin County Sheriff's windbreaker.

Charity had both the bow and stern lines in her hand as she stood on the gunwale, gripping the edge of the T-top with her free hand. When Mike maneuvered the boat close enough, she stepped over to the dock and quickly made the lines fast.

The three men climbed out of the boat, two of them assisting the man whose son was now dead. He rushed to a woman Charity assumed was his wife and the whole crowd swallowed them, moving toward the house.

Mike shut off the engines and stepped over. "What happened, Maggie?"

"You'll know in an hour or so, anyway," she replied. "Apparent drug overdose. Happened just before noon. The mother found him convulsing and unresponsive."

Mike ran his fingers through his hair, holding it for a second.

"That's crazy. This ain't that kinda town."

Brenda had told Charity once that she volunteered three days a week at the local police station, helping in the dispatch office. So Mike was no stranger to the police in such a small town, where everyone knew everyone else.

The sheriff's lieutenant looked over at Charity, as if seeing her for the first time. "Ms. Styles? I didn't know you were out with them."

"Please just call me Charity," she said. "I was a last-minute replacement for Brenda."

"She's been having false labor pains," Mike explained. "And the cramping makes her throw up."

"What time did you pick up Mr. Reynolds and his party?" Maggie asked, ignoring, or maybe understanding what Brenda was going through.

"Nine o'clock. Why?"

"Just gathering all the facts," Maggie said. "And you were on the boat all day?"

"Yeah, out past the ten-fathom line, mostly. About eleven miles offshore. We raced in when we got within cell range and Angelo—er, Mr. Rossi—got a text from his wife."

"Okay, thanks," Maggie said, then turned and nodded at Charity before starting up toward the house.

"Hey, Maggie," Mike called after her.

She stopped and turned back to face us.

"What about their fish?" he asked.

She looked up toward the grieving family. "I don't think they're going to miss them."

Mike stepped back down into the boat and restarted the engines, then looked up at Charity, waiting on the dock. "Let's get out of here."

She undid the lines and stepped aboard, coiling each line as Mike moved the boat away from the dock. She joined him at the leaning post as he brought the boat up on plane, heading west and staying close to shore.

"A drug overdose?" Charity asked. "That kind of thing happen often around here?"

"Not very," he replied. "Sure, there's weed and underage drinking. I did my fair share before Brenda and I got married. But kids OD'ing? Last I heard was years ago when I was still in school. No, wait, that's not exactly right. A Carrabelle girl overdosed a week ago. But I don't know what from."

Carrabelle was even smaller than Apalachicola, and twenty miles up the coast. Charity doubted the two incidents were connected.

"Do you know any of the details?"

He looked over at her for a moment. "Apparently, she died while partying with a local kid named Lucas Rivera and a bunch of others. I didn't really know either one. They were maybe ten years younger than me, but we all went to the same school."

"The same school?" she asked, thinking back to her own graduating class of nearly six hundred students.

"Franklin County School is all grades," he said. "And it's the only public school in the county. So, I went to school with people in the area who are twelve years younger than me to twelve years older—now fifteen to thirty-nine."

Charity thought about that for a moment, realizing it might be a large contributor to the cohesiveness of the people she'd met in the small towns she'd visited.

"Did you know the girl who died?"

"Karin Bishop," he replied. "A few years older than Lucas. Always a wild one. She ran off to L.A. a couple of years back and her boyfriend was popped for drug trafficking. She basically stole his car and drove back here."

As they approached *Wind Dancer*, Mike slowed the boat and brought it down off plane. Then, using the joystick, he maneuvered his boat alongside.

"You got room in your freezer for their catch?" he asked.

"Well, yeah, I guess so. You're not going to keep it?"

"Don't seem right," he vaguely replied, looking off to the east, where the rental house was. "If they call me and ask, maybe I could call you and you could run it over in your dinghy?"

Charity understood. Perhaps better than Mike did, himself. He was young, his parents likely not much older than Charity. He might even still have living grandparents, so he probably had little or no experience with death. He'd just seen the aftereffects firsthand, and what it did to others.

The dead boy's father had gone through several of the five stages of grief on the trip back. At first, he'd denied it, ranting that the police must have made a mistake. Then he'd grown quiet, moving away from the others in classic isolation. But it was difficult to be isolated on a small boat. The other men's consolations caused a brief flare of anger, the third stage, then he'd gone back to denial.

Charity had watched the man carefully, as well as his friends and Mike. She'd experienced death—up close, brutal, and personal. The fishermen, though all in their forties or fifties, had acted quite awkwardly with their friend.

Mike had concentrated on the water, his face a mask of urgency and fear. He didn't *want* to deal with death. Not while he and Brenda were bringing a new life into the world. That was why he was asking her to do this simple thing. To distance himself from it.

Charity touched his hand on the wheel. "Sure, Mike. I can do that."

After tying off, Charity went up and unlocked the companionway, noting the blond hair dangling where she'd left it. She helped Mike wrestle the cooler up onto her side deck and then down into the salon.

"Wow," Mike said, looking around. "I've never been inside a sailboat before. There's a lot of room."

"I thought you'd been around boats all your life."

"Shrimp boats and long-liners, yeah," he said. "But there aren't a lot of sailors around here."

"Modern sailboats have even more room," she said, opening the top-loading freezer and moving her stuff to one side. "Even things inside are made of fiberglass."

How old is your boat?"

"*Wind Dancer* was built almost ninety years ago," she replied. "All wood."

"Whoa," he said softly, looking around again. "I had no idea." He moved forward, slapping a hand on the thick wooden mast. "This goes all the way down to the bottom?"

"The mast is stepped on the keel, yes," she replied. "A Solid Sitka spruce log, just about a foot short of fifty feet long."

They bagged Mike's clients' catch, marking the plastic bags before putting them in the freezer. Then they carried the cooler back up the companionway.

The two stood in the cockpit for a second, Mike once more gazing out toward the east.

"Do you know how old the boy was?" she asked.

"Young," Mike replied. "Maybe fourteen or fifteen."

"Where could a fifteen-year-old kid on vacation buy drugs? It's doubtful he knew many people here."

Mike shrugged. "When I was fifteen, finding someone selling weed was easy."

"It had to have been either prescription drugs or heroin or meth."

He shrugged again. "Probably not that hard to find."

"Even in a town this small?"

When she'd first arrived, Charity had found the little downtown area to be quaint and charming, not a chain business anywhere. She'd thought it was almost like stepping into a Norman Rockwell painting.

"Yeah," Mike replied, "even in Apalach." He stepped up onto the side deck, then dropped lightly down into his boat. "Thanks again for helping."

"I'll get your lines," she said, as he started the outboards.

A moment later, Charity watched as Mike sped across the bay toward home. Then she went down into the salon and took a snapper fillet from the fridge for dinner.

Once back in her cabin, she rolled onto her bunk and stared up at the underside of the deck planks for a moment. Then she reached up, undogged the hatch, and pushed it open until it locked. The cool sea breeze caressed her face as she looked up at the top of her mast and a cloud drifting past.

How does a kid on vacation in a small town he's unfamiliar with wind up overdosing? What drug was it? Where did he get it? Who was in the supply chain?

All those questions mingled in the cop-trained part of Charity's mind as she stared up at the clouds. After leaving the Army, she'd accepted a job with Miami-Dade Police, working her way up from patrol officer to sergeant and becoming a martial arts instructor.

Then she wondered how the Franklin County Sheriff's Office was equipped to handle such crimes. Did they have a drug interdiction section? How big was the drug problem? How big was the police force?

She glanced over at the bowl and its inscription. Then she closed her eyes and took a deep breath, exhaling slowly.

"Ahoy, *Wind Dancer,*" a voice called out.

Charity's eyes opened and she was on her feet instantly, the handgun from under her pillow appearing in her hand. The voice had been strange, but somewhat familiar.

"Identify yourself!" she shouted up through the porthole, then added, "I am armed."

"It's Jojo," came the reply.

Charity put the DB9 in her pocket, then hurried aft and climbed up to the cockpit. Jojo was on a small sailboat, standing by the tiller easing the mainsail halyard to drop the sail to the deck as the boat slowly drifted toward *Dancer's* starboard side.

As the craft came alongside, Jojo turned and faced her. "I was wondering if you might like to go for a sunset sail?"

CHAPTER EIGHT

The two of them sat in *Wind Dancer's* cockpit, talking as the sun drifted lower and lower in the sky. She'd told him about the fisherman's son who'd overdosed and how Mike had been in a hurry to distance himself from what happened.

"I take it he's a young man?" Jojo asked.

"Maybe twenty-eight," she replied. "He and his wife are expecting their first child in a couple of months."

"Ah, I see. It is very understandable then, for him to not want to be around or become involved in such things. But what about you? How are you dealing with what happened?"

Charity looked blankly at him for a moment, trying to see beneath his calm exterior. He seemed genuinely concerned about how the death of a stranger had affected her. He had no idea he was sitting next to someone who'd snuffed out the lives of more than a dozen people.

"I've experienced death," she said flatly. "I used to be a cop."

His expression and demeanor didn't change, but his pupils constricted slightly. "I am sorry that you experienced those things, but we all do at some point. It is how we manage and move on that is important. When you were a police officer, there were probably mechanisms in place to help you to deal with the emotions."

"I've talked to my share of shrinks," she said without thinking.

His left eyebrow came up slightly. "Oh?"

She gave him another blank stare, assessing the man. Nothing about him gave any indication of strength or having overcome adversity, except his dark-brown eyes. She saw a depth and intensity there. He was a small man in both height and weight, but behind his eyes, Charity saw great willpower. In his culture, maybe being small didn't equate to being weak.

"Before becoming a cop, I was a medevac helicopter pilot in Afghanistan," Charity said slowly, going for the shock. "My bird was hit by a rocket and crashed. The enemy found us, and the helpless injured men in my helo were systematically gunned down. The Taliban held me captive in a filthy cave for three days as I was beaten, tortured, raped, and sodomized several times a day."

She delivered the lines stone-faced, as she had several times before with others. Most people quickly found a reason to be somewhere else.

Jojo's eyes grew a little moist as he searched her eyes. But he didn't turn away or run. "You carry a heavy burden," he finally said. "What happened to the men in your care had nothing to do with you. You were helpless to save them."

Charity blinked, her own eyes growing moist. He'd said it. He understood. All the psychologists and psychiatrists she'd seen after the incident in Afghanistan had all been primarily concerned with what had happened to her, physically, as a captive and how it had affected her mental state. Those who'd asked about the events leading up to her capture barely touched on what had happened to the men who'd died that day and how she'd felt about that. She'd locked the images of each man's face in her mind as they stared bravely at the Taliban fighter with the scar, just before he and his men shot them.

She turned her face away from Jojo, toward the setting sun, marveling at the colors as she sat silently. "Thank you," she quietly whispered.

"*Tomake shagôtô janai*," he said to her back. "It is the Bengali equivalent of 'you are welcome,' but it means much more."

As Charity gazed at the setting sun, a tear slowly traced its way down her cheek.

"Do you really have a gun?" Jojo asked. "Or did you say that just to frighten me away?"

Charity laughed and wiped her face. "I have several guns on my boat."

"What are you afraid of, Charity Styles?"

She turned to face him, the mask returning, as she squared her shoulders. "Nothing," she replied. "Absolutely nothing at all."

"Would you like for me to leave you alone?" he asked.

"No," she quickly replied. "I ruined your sunset sail. Let me make you dinner."

"You do not—"

"I insist," she said. "Do you like fish?"

It suddenly dawned on her that Jojo and The Buddha had eaten chicken the night before. She thought that was forbidden in Hindu practice and asked him about it.

"Daljeet and I have both lived here for most of our lives," he said. "He was a professor of eastern philosophy at UCLA. As an adolescent, I sneaked behind my parents' backs to meet other kids at burger joints. I'm afraid The Buddha and I have adopted a lot of Western culture." He smiled. "Me, a bit more so, perhaps. The cow is sacred in our culture, but the meat of fish or chicken is more acceptable. My spirituality is just that. It is how my mind works and processes things in the world. I am more a product of Southern California. I also enjoy kite surfing and burritos on the beach."

She smiled, then looked back toward the setting sun, now almost gone. "My father used to ask me if I could hear the sun sizzle at this time of day."

He followed her gaze as Charity closed her eyes for a second to make her wish. When she opened them again, the last of the sun disappeared over the horizon.

"The sun is sizzling somewhere on Earth every minute of every day," Jojo said. "Whether one hears it is more dependent on the individual than the sun. And far more indicative of a higher spirituality. Do you hear it?"

"I did when I was a girl," she said, rising. "And I've heard it as an adult on rare occasions. Come below. We'll cook together."

He followed her down into the salon. "I have wine," she said. "Or water."

"Wine, thank you," he said, looking all around the boat's interior, finally stopping at the open forward stateroom. "I see you have found a suitable place for it."

She looked in the direction he indicated. "Something happened last night."

"You made your bowl sing."

"Yes," she replied. "On the foredeck. And I slept there all night."

"Was it restful sleep? Uninterrupted by dreams?"

"Very," she said, as she opened a can of green beans and added them to a steaming pot. "And I wasn't sore when I woke up, which seemed very odd, sleeping nude on a hard deck in the cool night air."

His eyes sparkling a bit at that revelation, he moved over to a rack hanging on the wall to study Charity's collection of spices. "Very eclectic," he said, taking two small containers and moving over beside her.

"Is that a polite way of calling me a hoarder?"

"Not at all," he said, putting the spices down and glancing around the salon once more. "You are a highly organized person. You choose things that bring you comfort." He took another spice container from the rack and placed it with the first two, then picked up one of the pillows from the settee. "These are Polynesian, and that basket hanging there is Aboriginal. The sheets on your bed look like silk. From the Orient?"

"Brazilian," she replied. "But I was once told that their silkworms come from the same moths that were domesticated in China centuries earlier."

He turned back to the counter, where the large fish fillet lay on a cutting board. "You were going to eat all this yourself?"

"I usually cook two meals at once," she replied. "What's left is lunch for the next day."

Jojo held up one of the spice containers. "May I?"

"Please do," she replied.

He set them by the cutting board, then washed his hands at the sink and dried them on a towel hanging on the oven handle.

"I will need a sharp knife," he said.

"Top drawer, left of the stove," she replied, as she finished peeling a zucchini and began slicing it.

Using a slim knife, Jojo began cutting the fillet into strips. Then he opened one of the containers—Charity couldn't see which one—and took a large pinch, sprinkling it liberally over the fish. After repeating the process with the second container, but using a lot less, he put the two spices away and left the third one on the counter.

"Do you have a skillet?" he asked, looking around. "And a light cooking oil?"

Charity squatted and lifted a section of the deck, then retrieved her cast iron skillet from one of the many storage places below the deck planks.

"Anything heavy," she said, handing it to him, "I store below the sole for added ballast."

Then she reached under another section and produced two bottles, one of white wine and the other, coconut oil.

He took the wine bottle and looked at the label. "Caymanian," he said, pronouncing it correctly.

Most Americans pronounced the name of the island nation like it rhymed with bun. But down there, they pronounced it almost like caveman, without the V—cay man.

"I used to live on Grand," she said. "And *Dancer* and I have sailed to French Polynesia, Brazil, and Australia, among many other places."

Jojo put the skillet over a medium flame and added just a few teaspoons of the coconut oil as Charity moved the sliced zucchini into the steamer and added several small cherry tomatoes.

When the oil in the skillet started to sizzle, Jojo laid the strips of fish in side by side, then quickly turned each one over with a pair of tongs Charity handed him. He opened the third spice container and sprinkled a small pinch over the fish and into the oil, then flipped them again and did the same on the other side.

The two ate their dinner at the small dinette. The combination of spices and the coconut flavor were exotic and delicious.

"Why did you come here?" Charity asked, as they washed dishes next to one another.

"I thought you might like to go for a sail," he replied with a shrug. "I know sailing a large boat like this is enjoyable but takes much preparation. My little O'Day can be ready to go in seconds."

"I meant here in Apalachicola," she said.

He looked over at her and smiled. "To meet you."

Charity glanced at him doubtfully. "The two of you flew all the way from New York to meet me?"

"Not *just* that," he replied. "Though it has been the high point of our trip." He glanced away for just a fraction of a second. "I had business to discuss with Rudy."

That seemed slightly off to Charity, but she didn't press the point. The man was Rudy and Heather's spiritual advisor and he and The Buddha owned a successful school in Manhattan, so of course, there was business involved, and Rudy *was* a successful businessman.

A quid pro quo, maybe?

"I enjoyed the dinner very much," Jojo said, squatting to put the skillet away. He glanced up and smiled. "As well as the company."

Charity was ready to counter his advances with the lie about a bad breakup. She liked the man but wasn't interested in pursuing anything physical.

But if he persisted, she had other means at her disposal that would dissuade any man.

He stood and faced her. "But I'm afraid that I really must be going."

"Where do you keep your boat?"

"Battery Park Marina," he replied. "I enjoy the smaller boats and have several, each in a different location."

She followed him up the companionway to the cockpit. They'd tied the little daysailer alongside and he stepped over to it, standing on the port bench.

"You really must let me take you sailing around the island before Daljeet and I have to leave," he said. "She is not so grand a vessel as *Wind Dancer*, but there are many places my little boat can go that you cannot."

"What's her name?" Charity asked, as she untied his stern line.

"*Arva*," he replied, pushing the tiller over to bear away from *Wind Dancer*. "It means *From the Seashore*, as it is unlikely that she will sail far from it."

He went forward and untied the bow line, pushing away slightly before returning to the cockpit.

"*Arva* has no engine?" Charity asked, as Jojo began hoisting the mainsail in the darkness.

With the tiller over to port, the wind and current pushed the little boat back and away. Once the wind angle was great enough, the sail popped and *Arva* began sailing away at an angle, heading toward the lights of Apalachicola on the other side of the bay.

"She has no need of one," he called back in the darkness.

Charity watched as the little boat heeled slightly, gathering speed. She wondered how he'd maneuver the boat into a slip with no engine, but assumed he had a paddle and boat hook aboard. Still, doing it at night with no power or lights would require a good bit of skill.

Arva quickly disappeared against the blackness of the water. The tiniest sliver of a crescent moon hung barely above the horizon, casting insufficient light to catch the elusive little boat.

Charity looked around at the calm, still water surrounding her boat. In the direction Jojo had gone, she could hear nothing—no loose halyard, bouncing tackle, or slicing bow wave. Just silence. Then a high ringing sound rose and fell, as if carried on small waves.

Charity smiled, realizing that Jojo was using a singing bowl as a sort of a navigation aid or foghorn. She imagined him sitting on the bench with his foot on the tiller and a bowl in the palm of his hand. Would he have his eyes closed, listening for faint echoes?

The VHF inside crackled and she heard Mike's voice calling her.

She had two radios; one was kept on the international hailing frequency so she could hear any alerts or updates from Coast Guard Sector Mobile, two hundred miles away, or the nearby Pensacola station. She kept the second radio on Channel Seventeen.

After heading quickly down the steps, she plucked the mic from the second radio's holder. "*Wind Dancer* here. You okay, Mike?"

"Can you call me?" he asked.

"Give me your number," she replied, pulling her phone from her pocket.

She entered the number as he gave it, repeated it back, and when he confirmed, she hit the *Call* button.

"What's up?" she asked when he answered the call.

"I didn't want to say it over the radio, but I've learned a few things."

"A few things concerning what?" she asked, climbing back up and sitting on the port bench with her back against the cabin.

"Where that kid might have gotten the drugs," he replied. "The word on the street is, there's a lot of opioids suddenly floating around."

"Have you told the police? Your friend Maggie?"

"They know," Mike replied. "Brenda told me they've had a lot of calls about it, and a small, Hispanic-looking man is known to be selling stuff."

Charity looked off in the direction Jojo had disappeared. She could no longer hear the high-pitched ringing. "Well, that describes a good bit of the working-class population north of town."

Up the Apalachicola River, there were wide-spread farms and groves, worked mostly by migrants.

"Except this guy is always well-dressed and driving a flashy car," Mike said. "At least that's the description the cops are going off of."

"Do the police here have a drug interdiction team or anything like that?" she asked, still looking off toward the small town where Jojo had headed.

"I don't think so," he replied. "There's only about ten of them, including the chief."

"What about Franklin County?"

"Maybe three dozen deputies and as many office workers. We're a pretty small community here."

"Yeah, one school, I get it," she said. "Any connection to the girl who died last week?"

"Same drug," Mike said. "Prescription oxycodone."

"Well, I hope they catch the guy," Charity said.

She didn't believe they would for a minute, and even if they did, another one would appear almost immediately. The drug problem in the United States overwhelmed law enforcement everywhere.

They talked for another minute, then said goodbye, and Charity ended the call. She wondered why he'd found it necessary to tell her what was going on, but guessed it was because she'd asked so many questions.

Gazing up, Charity found the Big Dipper, its pointer stars angling at about thirty-degrees toward the North Star. Its position told her it was about ten o'clock, which she confirmed by checking the brass clock on the far wall when she descended the companionway steps.

She closed the overhead hatch and latched it, leaving the small doors open below it to allow for ventilation. There was a chance of rain, but with the bow pointing to windward, little would get in. Whatever did would end up in the bilge and be pumped out. The double doors were so small it would be nearly impossible for anyone to gain entry, unless they were on their belly.

Walking forward, Charity doused the lights, removed her

clothes and deposited them in the basket inside her hanging locker. Then she stripped out of the one-piece and stepped into the shower.

Ten minutes later, she emerged and toweled off, then slipped under the silk sheets in her bunk. She lay there staring up at the sky, hoping it wouldn't rain. Though she knew the scent of an approaching rainstorm would wake her and she could close the hatch before it started. It would mean the cabin would get stuffy and warmer than was comfortable, but she'd worry about that when and if it did.

She glanced over at the bowl, resting on its blue velvet cushion but didn't want to spend the night on the foredeck again, not with rain in the forecast. And she somehow sensed the bowl was an outdoor thing—a tool for meditating while sitting on the grass or on the beach.

For a few minutes, Charity stared up at the great spruce mast and rigging, pointing up to the stars. Her thoughts circled back to Jojo and The Buddha, who were both dark-skinned and well-dressed, but The Buddha could never be described as a small man. He wasn't tall, a couple of inches shorter than Charity's five-nine, but he was easily three hundred pounds.

Jojo, on the other hand, *was* small, even shorter than The Buddha. Charity guessed he couldn't possibly weigh much more than her own 135 pounds. At a distance, he might appear to be Hispanic.

She pushed the notion aside. He was simply too nice a person. Her last thought as she drifted off to sleep was how coincidental it was that the two had arrived about the same time as the sudden opioid epidemic.

CHAPTER NINE

Charity woke early the next morning, before dawn. She put on a sports bra, loose running shorts, sneakers, and her fanny pack, then took her dinghy to the Haverstocks' pier.

Once on dry land, she walked around the house to her car and leaned against it to do her stretching exercises. There was a black BMW sedan parked next to her Fiat; the badge on the back showed it to be an M760i. It looked awfully expensive.

The car wasn't Rudy and Heather's. Unless they'd traded their Land Rover. Besides, they wouldn't have parked it outside, so it had to belong to a visitor.

After stretching for a few minutes, Charity ran down Sawyer toward the highway. Crossing it, she continued down 11th Street to the beach.

The loose sand of the dune slowed her a little as her feet churned through it, but she soon reached the hard-packed part of the beach closer to the water's edge. On an impulse she turned left, running toward the rising sun.

Again, thoughts of the boy who'd overdosed crossed her mind. The rental house the three families were staying at was in that direction. They'd probably still be there, waiting for the boy's body to be released by the medical examiner.

The police were looking for a well-dressed Hispanic man who was small and drove a flashy car. In her experience most drug dealers did. For whatever reason, most criminals, especially drug dealers, relished showing off by buying cars they otherwise couldn't afford.

Are Jojo and The Buddha staying with the Haverstocks? Was it Jojo's flashy car she'd seen?

It was doubtful. They were from New York and had flown down. Few rental car companies had BMWs available.

I enjoy the smaller boats and have several, each in a different location, he'd told her.

Couldn't he as easily have several cars, so he'd have ground transportation available in the places he spent a lot of time?

But Charity had been anchored near her friends' house for six months. If Jojo was a regular visitor, she'd have seen him before now.

It seemed like it'd be a waste to have an expensive car like that and only drive it a couple of times a year. She made a point of trying to read the odometer when she got back.

The beach belonged to Charity. It was early and a weekday, so the majority of the fulltime residents of St. George Island were pouring coffee and getting dressed for work. Vacationers were likely still asleep.

The rhythmic slap of her shoes on the fine, hard-packed sand allowed her mind to drift, and she pondered her own situation, running from someone who might not even be interested in finding her. She'd done that a few times over the years. But like her friend Jesse would say, being paranoid didn't mean there *wasn't* anybody after you.

After she'd been in the area for a couple of months, Charity had contacted a friend who worked at Owen Roberts International

Airport on Grand Cayman. He'd told her that as far as he could see, her helicopter was still in its hangar, but beyond that, he didn't know.

The very next day, she'd driven all the way to Mobile, Alabama, bought a prepaid, throwaway cell phone, minimizing the chance it could be traced, and called the fixed base operator where her bird was stored.

The agent had seemed genuinely happy to hear from her. She'd told Charity the FBO's mechanic had taken the Huey out every Wednesday and started it up, just as Charity had asked. Her bill was current—paid every month through a numbered account at a bank on the island. She'd asked if anyone had inquired about her or the helo and was told a few people had asked about charters but other than that, nothing.

So, she'd hired a pilot to fly it to Tampa. She'd paid a lot extra for him to do it without asking questions. Then she'd allowed the bird to be stored for another three weeks before renting a car one-way and personally going down to check it out.

Charity knew a thing or two about tracking devices and how to find and remove them. She'd found only the one she herself had installed before leaving Grand. She'd then paid an exorbitant amount of money to a shady character to switch the tail numbers to those of a similar UH-1 Iroquois that was no longer serviceable. After that, she'd simply flown off in her bird and disappeared once more. Now the Huey was kept at St. George Island Airport, visible from her anchorage.

She hadn't flown it but twice since then, and nobody had come looking at it or asking about it. The helo belonged to her. It'd been transferred to her name, just like *Wind Dancer*, before the Caribbean Counterterrorism Command had been disbanded.

Either nobody was looking for her in connection with the death of Eisenstein, or Stockwell wasn't keeping an eye on her assets. Nobody, not even Stockwell, knew about the twenty-five million in Brunei currency she had stashed aboard her boat.

With that kind of money, plus what was in the Cayman numbered accounts—money she'd inherited from her father and had added to over the years—she could buy a fleet of helicopters. Boats, too, *and* have a car like the little Spider in every port. She could have plastic surgery to change her appearance and a new ID; then Charity Styles would cease to exist.

With that kind of money, she could do all that and more. Why didn't she? Why had she gone to such lengths to have Chyrel make a second phony entry in the DOT database and create a second driver's license with her real name on it? Was she that attached to her name?

There were probably a lot more people looking for her than just her past employer, though it didn't look like Armstrong was all that interested. Her name, picture, or some code word representing her was on a number of target lists. She'd made many enemies along the way.

Then there were others. Men she'd lured into her bed, some with wives and families. Charity felt no remorse about them. She'd only been satisfying her needs and they'd all been willing partners. She was sure more than one woman wished her dead. Maybe a few jilted lovers, as well. But most of them lacked the ability to find her, and more importantly, the ability to harm her.

Charity lived and worked alone. For the most part, she preferred not being around other people. She'd seen firsthand the darker side of humanity—those who would stop at nothing to gain the power and riches they wanted. And she'd encountered some who were just pure evil, men usually, who inflicted pain and suffering on others just for their own sick amusement. Eisenstein had been one of those. They came in all shapes and sizes, from every race, religion, nationality, and gender.

Evil didn't discriminate.

"Miss, wait!" a voice behind her shouted.

Charity stopped and wheeled around. In a flash, her left hand opened the small pouch at her waist, and the right one drew the compact DB9 handgun. When the gun came up, her feet were planted, and the sights were centered on the chest of a man coming toward her. He was one of the men from the previous day's fishing charter, the older one—the president of the law firm.

His hands came up and he stopped in his tracks, almost tripping as he back-pedaled. "Whoa, wait! Don't shoot! I'm unarmed."

Charity lowered the muzzle, pointing it at the sand in front of the man's feet. She stood and waited, her gun in the low ready position.

"Holy shit!" the man said, slowly lowering his hands. "Is that how you greet everyone?"

"Is there something I can do for you, sir?" she asked in an even tone.

He took a hesitant step closer. "I saw you running. You *are* the woman from the boat yesterday, right? Captain Rostock's friend? I mean no harm."

Charity put the handgun away but didn't zip the fanny pack. As she took two steps closer, remaining well out of arm's reach, she noticed a woman on the deck behind the man. She was wearing a floral print robe, and her hands flew to her mouth, as if she were about to scream.

"Yes, I was with you yesterday," she said, loud enough for both of them to hear. "I'm sorry about your friend's loss."

"Are you a police officer?"

"I used to be," Charity replied, closing the zipper. "I'm sorry. You surprised me."

"The police here...well, they're not telling us much. My name's Conti, Angelo Conti." He looked up at the woman, who'd taken one step down from the deck. "That's my wife, Gina."

He was in his fifties, if Charity had to guess, with dark, wavy hair, graying at the temples. His wife looked to be about the same age and also didn't try to hide her gray. A typical Italian-American couple from the suburbs, except for the Southern accent. She remembered Mike telling her they were from just outside Atlanta.

"It's normal during an investigation," she told the man, speaking quietly in case the boy's parents were listening. "Until the investigation is complete, they'll only release what information's necessary to the family."

The wife had slowly moved down the steps and stood slightly behind and to her husband's left. "Jeff wasn't a drug addict," she said. "He was a good kid, on the dean's list."

Charity looked past the man at Gina. Closer, she could see the lines in her face and the puffy red eyes. She'd been crying, or maybe hadn't gotten enough sleep. Probably both. Charity couldn't imagine what it must be like to lose a child, as she had none. This couple was enduring it right along with the boy's parents. She glanced up at the house. Three couples and half a dozen kids, all in one house, waiting.

"I'm sure he wasn't," Charity said. "This must all be quite difficult."

Gina took a step closer. "Do you have children, Miss...?"

"Just call me Charity," she said to the woman. "No, I don't have children."

"It's the worst thing that's ever happened," Angelo said, taking his wife's hand and pulling her close. "We're supporting Al and Dot as best we can. But like Gina said, Jeff wasn't into drugs. I seriously doubt he took drugs of his own volition."

Charity had worked quite a few drug-related cases with Miami-Dade PD, many of them involving teenagers and adolescents. The parents were always in denial.

"His wasn't the only overdose," she divulged, not knowing why. "A local girl died last week."

"That's horrible," Gina said, as her husband dropped his head and shook it sadly.

Finally, he looked up at her again. "Were you a police officer here?"

"No," Charity replied. "In Miami."

"But you know how these things work?" he asked. "They're saying it'll be several more days before they can release Jeff's body. Is that normal?"

"There's nothing normal about the death of a kid," she said. "You're a lawyer, right?"

"We specialize in probate law," he replied. "Wills, legacies, trusts. We almost never interact with police."

"The local police department here is small," Charity said. "Only a handful of officers in Apalachicola and a few dozen with the sheriff's office. It's just not something they're used to dealing with."

"You dealt with things like this a lot in Miami?" he asked.

Charity nodded somberly. "And a lot worse."

"Can I hire you?" Angelo asked. "We have nobody to turn to here."

CHAPTER TEN

As Charity came running up to the Haverstocks' house, Jojo was about to get into the BMW parked beside her car. When he saw her approaching, he stopped.

"If I'd known you were going for a run," he said, "I'd have asked to join you."

"Nice car," she said, looking into the interior.

The dash was blank, probably all electronic, so she couldn't tell how many miles were on the odometer.

"Thank you," he said. "I must say, yours is very nice as well. Not quite what I expected to see you driving."

"Oh? And what would you have expected?"

"Sorry," he said. "I meant nothing by that. I would have guessed you'd be driving something economical and sensible."

"I'll take that as a compliment," she said, running a hand over the back of the driver's seat of his expensive sedan. "To be honest, it wouldn't have been my first choice when I bought it. But the salesman offered to let me drive it and I fell in love. This is genuine leather?"

"The finest," Jojo replied. "You may get in, if you would like."

She smiled and slid behind the wheel. The seat was too far forward for her height, but it was comfortable, nonetheless.

Jojo touched a button on the key fob and the engine sprang to life, rumbling quietly.

"I bought it a couple of years ago," he said. "As one who appreciates performance, you'd enjoy driving it. The engine is a 6.6

liter, twin-turbo V-12, producing six hundred horsepower, with an eight-speed automatic transmission, and all-wheel drive."

Charity looked at the gauges. The odometer had less than ten thousand miles on it—incredibly low miles for a two-year-old car. She climbed out and gave Jojo a fake but sincere-looking smile.

"Probably way out of my price range," she said. "Are you and The Buddha staying here with the Haverstocks?"

He nodded as they exchanged places next to the driver's door. "For a few more days. We're flying to L.A. on Friday."

"So, you didn't drive this magnificent machine down from New York?"

"We travel too much to drive anywhere," he replied. "I keep the car stored at a garage over on the mainland. As with my boats, I have several cars, also strategically located. After L.A., we're flying to Bangladesh for a week or two."

"When did you get here?" she asked, since he'd brought up the subject of traveling.

"Over two weeks ago," he replied. "Daljeet met with several of our followers here, while I took a week to drive to Pensacola and meet with business associates. So, really, I've only been here for a little over a week. Rudy and Heather were kind enough to allow us use of their guest wing."

"They have a whole guest wing?"

Charity had been in the house several times, but only the living and kitchen areas.

He smiled and leaned closer. "They like to refer to it as such. The two downstairs bedrooms on this side of the house, separated by a restroom."

Charity made a move toward the side of the house. "It was nice seeing you again. I have to get back to my boat."

"The pleasure was mine," he said, bowing slightly. "I am always at the disposal of such a beautiful woman."

Charity turned and walked quickly around the house. "I just bet you are," she mumbled under her breath.

ELUSIVE CHARITY

Once back aboard *Wind Dancer*, Charity got out of her sweaty clothes and tossed them in the basket, noting that she'd have to make a laundry run very soon. She didn't want to impose on Heather and ask to use her machines; it was nice enough of them to allow her to use their dock and driveway to come and go.

She turned on the hot water and stepped into the shower. The small water heater only held twenty gallons, but that was more than enough for a good pore-opening and final rinse. She used unheated water from the sea to lather up as she considered what she'd learned.

The two men had arrived in Apalachicola two weeks ago and Jojo had driven to Pensacola on business in his flashy black car with very low miles, then he'd returned just about the time of the girl's overdose last week.

For a two-year-old car, it had exceptionally low miles. But for a car that was only driven a couple of times a year over the last two years, it actually had pretty high mileage.

If she could assume he'd been to Apalachicola five times since he'd bought the car, and also assuming it had close to zero miles when he'd purchased it, that was just under two thousand miles of driving for each visit. She couldn't see anyone driving that much just around the small town. But if he'd driven all over the Florida Panhandle and South Georgia, that much mileage was possible.

The timing of the girl's death and Jojo and The Buddha's arrival was a thin veil of a coincidence at best—what Deuce would have called a reach. If that was all she looked at.

But coupled with the description of the drug seller and his car, she was beginning to wonder if Jojo hadn't gone to Pensacola to pick up prescription drugs to sell in Carrabelle and Apalachicola. Or maybe he was covering a much larger area, using fake prescriptions at dozens of pharmacies. Then again, it might just as easily be that he simply liked driving.

How much profit could there be in a meditation school?

Profit was one of two things that nearly every crime eventually came down to. When she'd worked with Deuce's team, a man named

Paul Bender had been a part of it. He'd been a former Secret Service agent, on the presidential protection detail, no less. But he'd also earned a degree in forensic psychology. He'd explained to the team that understanding criminal motivation wasn't difficult.

"When you strip away all the layers of sub-motivation," he'd once said, "it almost always comes down to one of two things—love or money."

Turning off the hot, steamy water, Charity stepped out of the head and dried off, then she bent over and hung her hair down, wrapped it in the towel, gave it a twist and flipped it over her shoulder.

She'd promised Angelo Conti that she'd look into things and see if she could learn any details about Jeff's death or who the drug dealer might be.

At the moment, she was leaning toward Jojo.

Opening her laptop, she connected to the Haverstocks' Wi-Fi—another benefit of anchoring behind her friends' house—and started a search for Oxycontin, one of the most prevalent prescription opioids in most American cities.

On the streets, it could sell for as much as twenty dollars for a single five-milligram tablet. Buying it legitimately at a licensed pharmacy with a doctor's prescription, the cash price if you didn't have insurance was only about thirty cents. If a dealer could get his hands on a lot, spending a couple thousand dollars at pharmacies all over the area, he could sell them individually and make a profit of more than $130,000.

But multiply that initial investment by ten and there were suddenly over a million reasons to drive around to dozens of pharmacies all over the Southeast.

How many tantric meditation clients would it take to make that kind of money?

Charity stood and paced the deck as she thought—four steps from her stateroom to the galley and four steps back.

In Manhattan, maybe not that many. New York City was full of wealthy, uptight professionals looking for spiritual guidance and healing.

So, why come to Apalachicola? Or even Pensacola, for that matter. The city where Jojo had said he'd driven to on business and spent nearly a week was larger, but hardly a city of higher enlightenment. How many followers could Jojo and The Buddha have in small, Southern towns? And how profitable would it be to visit for two weeks, neglecting their devotees in New York? If the school existed and was doing well, she wouldn't think it would make much sense.

She then searched the Internet for Daljeet Khatri—The Buddha's real name—and quickly found the school. It was called Temple of Enlightenment and was located on the Upper East Side of Manhattan, a very affluent area, to say the least. The price for even a small apartment there was several million dollars and not much bigger than her boat. The more she dug, the more legit the school appeared.

But there was no mention of Jojo.

She opened another tab and tried searching for his nickname, along with several variations of his first name, and the last name Laghari. She finally found Jyotiraditya Laghari, a Manhattan investor.

She clicked on the *Biography* tab, located on the menu bar across the top of the page, and a picture of Jojo appeared, along with a brief bio.

He'd graduated UCLA in 1999 with a degree in philosophy. No surprise there. But then he'd gone on to earn a master's in finance at Berkeley two years later. He was forty-four years old, born in Bangladesh, and had immigrated with his parents to Los Angeles in 1983 at the age of five. In 1996, before starting college, he'd become an American citizen.

All information he'd freely divulged to her before dinner the other night. He was a public figure, hardly the drug dealer type. So, why no mention of him on the school's website?

She thought back to the night before last when she'd first met the two men. Jojo had said that The Buddha taught tantric meditation in a school in Manhattan, and she'd assumed it was *their* school.

Was Jojo the school's financier?

Looking at pictures of the school, it was obvious it was highly successful. Real estate in Manhattan wasn't cheap and the pictures were resplendent with tranquil indoor settings, even a meditation garden with a giant sun dome. Easily into eight figures.

As Charity looked at each image, she began to see drug money, framed and hanging among the tapestries.

CHAPTER ELEVEN

Charity needed some answers before she could even begin to ask any more questions. She wasn't sure why she'd agreed to help. The Contis had just seemed like such nice people, and their pain, even though they weren't related to the dead boy, was palpable.

Out on Mike's boat, she'd talked to all three men—just idle conversation lasting a few seconds here and there. They were three guys out for a day of fun. She'd enjoyed herself also.

As she dressed, she thought about going to Lieutenant Hamilton for some answers, but doubted she'd get any more information than what had already been given to the family. From her hanging locker, she chose a navy skirt and white blouse—one of the outfits she'd worn as a bartender on the yacht *Heart and Soul*. For what she was about to do, she didn't feel her typical boating attire would be suitable. Pulling the skirt up, she strapped her holstered DB9 handgun to the inside of her thigh, then smoothed the skirt back into place.

Charity wanted to know precisely what the drugs were that killed the two young people, and the dosage if possible. That meant starting at the hospital where both victims had undoubtedly been taken, George E. Weems Memorial.

Dressed and ready, she opened a secret compartment under the bunk and removed a small booklet, leafing through the plastic card-holder pages until she found what she was looking for. After removing a small ID card and putting it in her billfold, she grabbed her laundry bag and carried her shoes up to the cockpit, then deposited them in the dinghy. Before leaving, she remembered to nestle a strand of hair in the hatch.

Several minutes later, Charity was zipping across the short distance to Rudy and Heather's dock, where she tied off her dinghy and tossed her purse, laundry bag, and shoes up onto the planks and climbed out. As she took the walkway around the side of the house, she noticed that Jojo's car was still gone. She slid into her car, dropping the bag in the passenger seat, then quickly put the top down, wondering where he'd gone off to and if The Buddha was still at the house.

Though the town of Apalachicola was just across the bay, only five miles away, the drive was more than double that, including two bridges that were both four miles in length.

She drove at the speed limit into East Point, turned left, then pulled into the Wash and Fold. She left her laundry bag and a twenty-dollar bill with the attendant, asking her to please use cold water, then was back in her car and headed west across John Gorrie Bridge.

Topping the arched part of the bridge, she slowed and downshifted her Spider as she approached the curve. US-98 was elevated, and she could see down into Battery Park Marina, where Jojo had said he kept his boat. There wasn't a black sedan anywhere in the small parking lots.

She downshifted again, letting the engine slow the car as she entered the curve, and the bridge descended to ground level in the middle of town.

Continuing to follow her GPS, she turned onto Avenue E, shifting slowly up through the gears in light traffic. Several blocks and a couple of turns later, she pulled into the small hospital's parking lot.

It was doubtful that the autopsies were performed there—it was very small. More likely the bodies had been transferred to the medical examiner's office in Tallahassee, about eighty miles away. But she had to start somewhere.

Charity's assumption was confirmed when she asked at the hospital's reception desk if there was a coroner on staff and was told no.

She slid the card from her billfold and passed it to the middle-aged receptionist. "I'm investigating the death of Jeffrey Pender," Charity said. "Was there an attending physician who I might talk to?"

The woman looked at the fake Florida private investigator's license, complete with a license number that, when searched, would show her to be a bona fide PI in good standing. But just like her driver's license, it wouldn't come up in a name search.

The receptionist, who wore a nametag with just *Doris* printed on it, slid the license back across the counter. "You'll want to talk to Dr. Mandrote. He was the ER doctor on call the morning the boy was brought in."

"Would he know about the local girl who overdosed last week?" Charity asked, putting the card away. "Karin Bishop?"

"I'm not sure about that," the woman replied, turning toward her computer screen. "Let me check. Is there some connection between the two?"

"Not that I know of," Charity replied. "Aside from the fact they both overdosed. The boy was a vacationer. It was his father's law firm who hired me, and I figured since the COD was the same, I might have questions about both."

Doris looked up, puzzled. "CO... Oh, of course. Cause of death." She went back to her keyboard, pecking a few keys, then looked up. "Yes, Dr. Mandrote was the attending physician in the ER for both of them." She checked her screen again and announced, "You should find him in the cafeteria about now."

Charity looked at her watch. It was barely past ten.

"He's usually here before sunrise," the woman said, noting the unasked question. "That was when the girl was brought in. He takes a lunch break at ten o'clock and goes home at three. Then he comes back in to make rounds after dinner."

"Thank you," Charity said. "How will I find the cafeteria?"

The woman pointed past Charity's right shoulder. "Through

those doors and down the hall. It's on the left; you can't miss it. Look for a short, balding man with a beard."

"Thanks, again," she offered, then turned and headed toward the double doors, her low heels clicking evenly on the hard floor.

It was quite easy to find the cafeteria, and there were only three people sitting at three different tables—a man and two women. She approached the man, who looked to be about fifty and fitted Doris's description.

"Are you Dr. Mandrote?" she asked, pulling her fake PI license out again.

He stopped in mid-bite and put his sandwich down, then rose from his chair. "Yes, I am. How may I help you?"

Charity handed him the license. "My name is Charity Styles. I'm a private investigator looking into the death of Jeffrey Pender on behalf of the boy's family. I wonder if I might ask you a few questions?"

"Please have a seat," the doctor said, pulling out an adjacent chair. "I only have about twenty minutes for lunch. Will this take long?"

"Not at all," Charity replied, taking the offered seat. "Go ahead with your meal, Doctor. I only have a few questions."

He sat back down and took a small bite of his sandwich. "I gave a full report to the sheriff," he said. "Pretty simple case. The young man died of an overdose of prescription opioid."

"Were you able to determine which one and what quantity?"

"Definitely oxycodone," he replied, talking around a handful of potato chips. "The ME in Tallahassee did the autopsy, but I took a tox screen as soon as he was brought in unresponsive. From the results I found, along with the ME's report, I'd say the Pender boy ingested approximately twenty milligrams, most likely in the form of two ten-milligram immediate-release tablets."

"Why do you say that?"

"The coroner's report on the stomach contents," he replied, swallowing another bite. "The tablets hadn't even fully dissolved."

"Twenty milligrams is a lot," Charity said, remembering some of the oxy cases she'd worked in Miami.

"Indeed," the doctor agreed. "In immediate-release form, fifteen milligrams would be fatal to most adults. A ten-milligram tablet is usually prescribed only to patients who are much larger in size. The boy was barely a hundred pounds."

"I understand you were also on call when Karin Bishop was brought in. Can you tell me if she died from taking the same drug?"

"That was in my report to the sheriff also," he replied, then put down his sandwich and looked at Charity with a grave expression. "Yes, based on the same tests, findings, and stomach content examination, I'd say the girl also ingested at least two ten-milligram tablets, on top of having a blood alcohol level just under the legal limit and smoking cannabis. She was very petite, no bigger than an average thirteen-year-old girl. Because of that, as was likely the case with the Pender boy, she probably died within minutes of ingestion."

"Was there anything else unusual about either case?" Charity asked.

He looked down at his half-eaten sandwich, then pushed the plate aside, tenting his fingers and peering at Charity.

"I estimated the boy's time of death no more than an hour before the ambulance brought him in," Mandrote replied. "His liver temperature had dropped less than a degree. The girl's time of death was approximately eight to ten hours before she was brought in."

"Eight to ten hours?"

"I'd lean toward the latter," he replied. "Maybe even a bit longer. It was a hot night and the body had been in an enclosed vehicle."

"Did the police or sheriff's office find out what the delay was?"

"The boy she was with said he thought she'd just gotten into the back of his covered truck and fallen asleep."

"Your expression tells me you don't believe that."

He shook his head. "She had sex at about the same time she died."

CHAPTER TWELVE

Lucas looked up toward the bridge and ran the back of his forearm across his brow, wiping away the sweat. It was early May but already hotter than blue blazes. The sound of a high-revving engine downshifting had taken his attention away from the outboard he and Kenny were tinkering with.

A little blue convertible coming across the bridge was rounding the curve and quickly disappeared into downtown Apalach.

"You got as much chance of gettin' that as you do of gettin' this thing to crank," Kenny said, following his friend's gaze.

"If I had a car like that, I'd be outta this town in ten seconds," Lucas said.

"Car? You didn't even see the hot blonde driving it, did you?"

"Huh?" Lucas glanced over at his friend, then quickly bent back over the outboard. "I think it's not gettin' gas."

It'd been ten days since the party at the abandoned farm out on Highway 67. When he'd first realized that Karin was dead, Lucas had freaked out. He'd never seen a dead person. Then the slow realization hit him that she'd already been dead when he'd rolled off her. The thought that he'd had sex with a corpse had nearly made him throw up. Finally, he'd realized that nobody knew where they were. So, he'd redressed her, which wasn't difficult—she was super little and had worn only shorts and a tank top. Then he'd quietly slipped out of the back of the truck and locked it back up.

"No shit, it ain't gettin' no gas," Kenny said. "The tank's almost full and the ball's harder than your dick was while you was searchin' for Karin. So, somethin's blockin' the flow."

Lucas looked up, his dark eyes flashing with anger. "What'd you say?"

"Come on, man," Kenny said, grinning. "The whole town knows. You two were thrashin' and rollin' around down by the river like a pair of horny possums; then she went to sleep it off in your truck." Kenny snickered. "It was almost comical, man. You, runnin' around with your dick in your hand trying to find her for round two, and the whole time she was dead in your bed, man."

"It wasn't like that," Lucas said, a little too forcefully.

"Oh, yeah?" Kenny continued. "What *was* it like then?"

"Dude! She's dead!"

"Duh," Kenny retorted. "And wherever she ended up, you was her last lay, and she'll have all eternity to remember it."

"Fuck you, man!" Lucas said. "Now, you gonna help me figure out where the hell the fuel filter is on this thing or not?"

After getting out of the back of his truck that night, Lucas had circled around to the far side of the group around the fire before returning, as if coming back from the river. He'd intentionally let it slip that they'd been making out down by the river, and then just let nature take its own course. After an hour or so, he'd asked if anyone had seen Karin, then gone off to look for her. By the time she was found several hours later, everyone knew they'd done it, and some were even saying they'd heard them. He'd made sure that he was off looking for her again when Marc went to his truck to get more lighter fluid and discovered the body.

Lucas and Kenny went back to work on the engine and soon found the filter. They didn't have a replacement but cleaned the old one as best they could until they were able to get a new one. Once it was back in, the engine started after several pulls on the cord.

"Hell, yeah!" Lucas exclaimed.

Kenny raised his right hand for a high-five and then froze. Lucas watched his expression change as he noticed something over his shoulder. He turned around and saw Maggie Hamilton walking toward them.

"Uh-oh," Kenny said. "You got anything on ya?"

Lucas had a joint in his cigarette pack and his hand subconsciously moved to his shirt pocket. The lady cop's eyes caught the movement and flicked down for just a second.

"Hello again, Lucas," she said, stepping down onto the dock beside Lucas's old boat.

"More questions?" Lucas practically whined.

She glanced over at Kenny. "Get lost."

Kenny wasted no time and scrambled out of the boat, glancing back twice as he crossed the grassy area to the parking lot.

"No more questions, Lucas," the lieutenant said. "I'm here to give you some information and allow you a chance to change your story."

She reached into the inside pocket of her jacket and took out a piece of paper. "I have an order here, signed by Judge Thomas, telling me to get a sample of your DNA. Do you know what that is?"

Lucas hung his head. "You won't need no blood," he said. "Karin and I had sex before she disappeared. I didn't want to say anything, cuz I didn't want to...um..."

"Tarnish her sterling reputation?"

"Something like that," Lucas replied, without looking up.

"That boat left the bay a long time ago, Lucas. From what I can tell, you were the latest in a lengthy line. It might not be a bad idea for you to see your doctor."

CHAPTER THIRTEEN

Charity sat in her car in the hospital parking lot with the top down. A girl had died, and nobody'd noticed for the whole night. Because Jeff Pender had been a minor, Dr. Mandrote hadn't told her anything more than the basics about his case. He'd told her that he'd performed an initial exam of the girl's body and determined she'd had sex near the time of her death and he'd taken a swab for DNA testing.

She'd told the doctor that, unlike the press or the police, a private investigator wasn't obliged to divulge the source of their information or how it was obtained, nor did they need warrants. Private investigator meant just that—private. He'd told her that the DNA sample matched the young man the dead girl had been seen with that night, the kid Mike had told her about, Lucas Rivera. The police had a past sample on file, from a previous incarceration in the county jail, to compare it to and were sending someone to get a current sample.

Charity took her phone out and found Lucas Rivera's Facebook page easily enough. She scrolled through a bunch of out-of-focus profile pictures, mostly with more than one person in the shot, until she found one that showed his face clearly.

He looked younger than nineteen, with dark curly hair, onyx

eyes, and light-brown skin, which was somewhat expected considering his last name.

She committed his features to memory, then started the engine and pulled out of the parking lot, heading southeast on 12th Street. Without giving it a thought, she was absently moving toward water. She realized her mind was on autopilot when she turned left on Bay Avenue and could see the bridge.

Battery Park Marina was just ahead on the right and Charity slowed to see if Jojo's BMW was there. She could see most of the lot across the fairway. It was occupied primarily by older cars and trucks, as was the smaller parking area on Bay Avenue, which she was slowly creeping past.

A black Jeep Cherokee caught her eye as it pulled out of the lot on the other side of the marina, then drove under the bridge on Water Street.

What was Lieutenant Hamilton doing there?

Charity pulled into an empty spot on the Bay Avenue side of the marina and got out, watching the Jeep as it continued past the bridge toward the older downtown area.

She looked around the marina. Most of the boats looked unattended, some almost derelict. The Haverstocks' Hylas, *Bottom Line II*, docked across the fairway, was the crown jewel of the marina. Directly in front of it was a small O'Day sailboat. She could clearly see the name *Arva*, painted across the stern. In the last spot before the dock turned, the spot where she'd once docked *Wind Dancer*, there was a slightly larger sailboat, probably a little under thirty feet. Seeing the name, she assumed it was a twenty-seven-footer. *Whole Nine Yards* was emblazoned across the transom.

Clever name, she thought, also thinking she'd heard it before.

Where the long, right-angled dock met shore was a boat ramp.

A pair of young men were bent over the outboard of a small boat. Aside from them, she couldn't see anyone else around.

Had Maggie been there to question Jojo?

She got back into her little Spider and drove around to the other parking lot where Water Street curved under the bridge. That lot was mostly for vehicles with boat trailers, but being a Tuesday, there were only two pickups with heavy work trailers.

She'd check Jojo's boat and if he was there, she'd simply say she'd been in the area and wanted to thank him for helping her cook dinner.

Then she could subtly steer the conversation toward the lieutenant and her questions.

Getting out of her car, Charity started along the dock toward *Arva,* bobbing at the end before the dock turned. The two young men were sitting in their boat, the cover off the outboard motor. When they looked up, she immediately recognized Lucas Rivera.

Charity stopped and looked down at the two teenagers. She glanced toward Jojo's boat, then back at the two boys gawking up at her.

"Do either of you know Jojo?" she asked. "The man who owns the little O'Day sailboat at the end of this dock?"

"I've um...seen him around," Rivera replied. "D-don't know his name." He glanced past her at the parking lot. "Is that your car?"

Charity tossed her long, blond tresses over her shoulder and looked back. "The blue 124 Spider? Yes, it belongs to me." She looked down at the two again. "Have you seen Jojo today?"

"He was here this mornin'," the other boy said. "He left right after we got here."

"And you're sure he hasn't been back?"

"Been here all morning," Rivera's friend replied. "We'd have seen him walk by."

Of course, Charity thought, glancing over at the exit, where the cop had just left from. Lieutenant Hamilton herself had come to get the DNA sample.

She put her hands on her hips and looked straight at Rivera. "So, Lieutenant Hamilton was here to see you then, Lucas?"

"Huh? Say what?"

"She came to take a DNA sample, didn't she?"

"How the hell...?" Rivera stood up at the back of the boat. It rocked, but he showed no indication of being off-balance. "Who are you?"

He was slightly built, maybe a little over Charity's own weight, but not by much. A small, Hispanic-looking man.

"My name's Charity Styles," she replied. "I'm a private investigator, hired by the Conti Law Firm in Atlanta, to look into the death of one of the partner's sons—a fifteen-year-old boy named Jeff Pender. Does that name mean anything to you?"

The kid's face registered relief. And not in a subtle way. He practically blew out a "whew!"

"Never heard of him," the other young man said. "And we know just about everyone around here."

Charity fixed the young man with a blank gaze, as if he were nothing but a whining gnat at her ear. He was slightly taller and heavier than Rivera, with dark blond hair and the beginnings of a mustache.

"Yeah," she said. "Small town. One school. I get it. What's your name?"

"You're not a real cop," the other boy said, standing up suddenly. "I don't gotta tell you shit, lady."

The boat rocked again, but both of them easily countered it.

They were obviously no strangers to rolling decks.

Charity slowly squatted down until her butt met her heels and her eyes were on the same level as that of the two boys. Her skirt rode up slightly and the boys' eyes went wide when they spotted her holstered gun.

"That's right," she said, with a genuine-looking, lustful smile. "But before this gets all weird or kinky or anything, are both of you men over the age of eighteen?"

It had the desired effect. Both of their faces flushed, and she could read the animalistic urge in their eyes just from the mere mention of the word kinky. This was a pair of young American males, ready for anything, with testosterone raging out of control.

"We're both nineteen," Rivera said.

Charity looked at the other one and smiled. "You are absolutely correct. I'm not a cop. They have rules and can't do this."

Like a rattlesnake striking, Charity's right fist shot out and caught the other boy squarely in the forehead—a well-focused jab, meant to put the boy's lights out.

His eyes rolled back from the impact of the blow, but there hadn't been enough follow-through to cause his head to snap back. In fact, it barely moved a fraction of an inch before his legs buckled and he simply collapsed between the benches in the front of the boat.

Rivera stared down at his friend. He started to move toward him but stopped and looked back over to where Charity still squatted next to the boat, as if nothing had happened.

"You killed Kenny!"

Charity almost laughed until she realized the *South Park* line probably meant nothing to the young man.

"Kenny isn't dead," she said, her voice flat and cold. "If he'd just

101

answered my question instead of mouthing off, he wouldn't be waking up with a wicked headache."

"Who are you?"

"I told you," Charity said. "I'm a private investigator. And I don't like boys who mouth off or are disrespectful to women." She pouted, her lower lip almost trembling. "You're not going to be like that are you, Lucas?"

"No...um...no, ma'am."

Charity smiled. "That's good. Now, what did Maggie want with you? And before you answer, you should know that I often ask questions I already know the answers to." She shrugged nonchalantly. "You know, just to judge how open a person is being with me."

Rivera sat down and Kenny began to stir.

"She used a Q-tip in my mouth," he said. "I thought she wanted to draw blood, but she only needed my spit."

"To make a positive match to the DNA that was found on Karin Bishop's body?"

His head came up. "Yeah, but you said you were invest—"

"Jeff Pender died taking the same drug," Charity interrupted, glancing down at the knuckles on her right hand. A drop of blood fell to the planks from a small cut in her middle knuckle. She put it to her lips, tasting the coppery flavor of her own blood before dropping it back into place on her knee.

"Do you have a car, Lucas?"

Lucas stared at her hands resting lightly on both knees, which were parted just enough to reveal the barrel of the 9mm sticking out of the bottom of the holster.

Charity could see his mind racing, all sorts of fantasy role-playing activities likely dancing through his little adolescent head.

Then she saw fear, as he no doubt recalled how fast her hand had moved.

"No," he replied, then quickly added, "Well, yeah, sorta. I use my old man's pickup. He took off."

"What kind?"

"A Ford," Lucas replied. "A 1985 F-150."

Hardly a flashy vehicle, Charity thought, then switched gears. "Did *you* take oxy the night Karin died?"

There was a pause, and Charity shifted her weight ever so slightly, moving her left hand just enough to get his attention.

"Yeah! Yeah, I took one," he confessed. "Karin took two."

"And it was oxy, right?"

"Yeah, she said she'd done two at a time a bunch of times. I didn't think it'd make her OD."

"How'd it make you feel?"

"What do you mean?" he asked, the color draining from his face.

"Was it a normal high?"

He glanced around as Kenny moaned and slowly tried to get up to his hands and knees.

"Way higher," Rivera replied. "I figured it was just a really good batch or something like that."

"A good batch, huh?" she asked rhetorically, practically spitting the word out. "It's prescription medication, you moron. Made in a lab with precise ingredients."

"Look, I don't know nuthin' about how it's made."

"So, let me get this straight," Charity said. "You're telling me that neither of you knew the pills you took were the *ten*-milligram immediate-release tablets?"

"Huh?"

"It's the dosage, you fucking idiot!" Charity said, beginning to feel a cold rage building in her gut. "Ten milligrams! The pills you took were meant to instantly sedate a man twice your size. One pill!"

CHAPTER FOURTEEN

After calming herself, Charity had asked Lucas Rivera a few more pointed questions and knew there was more to his story than he was letting on. She could tell by his body language and his eyes. Something sickening or repulsive to him. If Maggie Hamilton were half the cop it took to make lieutenant with Miami-Dade, she would have picked up on it, as well. But Charity felt confident that neither Rivera nor his mouthy friend knew who Jeff Pender was. The fact that Karin and Lucas had likely bought the drugs from the same person was probably the only connection. Rivera had sworn he didn't know the man that Karin Bishop had arranged the buy with. Charity half-believed him but chose not to push it further. He'd clam up and beating him senseless wouldn't open his mouth. Drug users were usually very tight-lipped when it came to their suppliers.

She got back into her car and drove under the bridge, heading north on Water Street. The courthouse was in that direction; maybe that was where Hamilton had gone. After a couple of blocks, she saw the Cherokee parked in front of a place called Boss Oyster, which Charity had heard of many times since arriving, but had never tried.

There was a vacant gravel spot next to Lieutenant Hamilton's Jeep and she swung in. The lieutenant was just coming out, and she was with a very tall man who carried himself confidently. They stopped at the fender of her car and talked for a moment, then they kissed and he walked away, twisting the top off of a large, green soft-drink bottle and chugging it. When the lieutenant turned to get into her car, she saw Charity and paused.

Here's your big test, Chyrel, Charity thought, as she exited the little car, already pulling her fake PI license out of her billfold.

"I hope you've been keeping your speed down, Ms. Styles," Lieutenant Hamilton said, as Charity strode toward her.

"And keeping an eye out for your Cherokee, when I don't," Charity replied with a smile. "I don't suppose you could tell me if there are any other unmarked police cars, are there?"

Hamilton smiled back. "That's for us to know," she said. "What brings you off the island on such a beautiful morning?"

"Laundry," Charity answered. "I dropped a couple of loads off at the Wash and Fold over in East Point and figured I'd drive over here to see if I could find you."

Maggie's face became serious. "What can I help you with, Ms. Styles?"

"Do you have a few minutes?"

The lieutenant glanced down at the large coffee cup in her hand and swirled it around. Then she looked up the street where, on the other side, a coffee shop was located.

"Buy me a coffee at Kirk's and you have my ear," Hamilton said.

Charity handed the license to her. "I've been retained by the Pender family."

Hamilton looked down and examined the license, front and back, then handed it back. "I doubt I can tell you anything more about the boy's death than you already know from the Penders—it's an ongoing investigation. At least not enough to warrant the price of a cup at Kirk's."

"I'll take my chances," Charity said, as she reached across the open car and plucked her own travel mug from the cup holder. "Besides, I could use a refill."

The two women walked in silence across the street and then down the sidewalk toward the coffee shop. There were few cars and only an occasional passerby, each of whom nodded and called the lieutenant by her first name.

"I know you're aware that both Jeffrey Pender and Karin Bishop overdosed on the same prescription drug, oxycodone," Charity said, as they walked along.

"Yes, I do," Maggie said. "But that's not public knowledge."

"And I know you're looking for a small, Hispanic man who drives a fancy black car."

"Also not released to the public," Maggie said, as they turned left onto Avenue D, just before the coffee shop. "Where do you get your information?"

Charity noticed another coffee shop just half a block ahead.

"A PI's sources are confidential," she replied. "I don't want to step on your toes, Lieutenant. Or anyone else's. But I can't divulge my sources. At least, not yet."

They continued walking in silence, passing the second coffee shop, then turning onto Market Street, where Charity saw a third coffee shop, Apalachicola Chocolate and Coffee Company. Just like the other two, not a chain store, and all within a hundred yards of each other.

They went inside and ordered coffees from a severe-looking man behind the counter, who seemed surprised and a little irate to see Hamilton. Then they sat down at a table in the corner.

"The coffee must be very good here," Charity said, as they moved to a table in the corner. "We passed two other coffee shops in the short walk over here."

"I don't go to those anymore," Hamilton said.

Something in her eyes told Charity not to press the point—some sort of pain or a bad memory of those places.

"It's hard not to step on anyone's toes in a town as small as Apalach," the lieutenant said, looking directly at Charity. "Mr. Pender didn't mention anything about hiring a PI. That's who hired you, right?"

"Not exactly," Charity replied, knowing how cops and private investigators didn't exactly co-mingle a lot after hours. "Mr. Pender is a partner in the Conti, Marshall, and Pender Law Firm, up in Atlanta. The senior partner, Angelo Conti, retained my services."

"So, what can I tell you that you don't already know?"

"I'm new in town," Charity replied. "I was once in law enforcement down in Miami."

"I'm sure that was challenging work," Maggie said, taking a sip.

Charity nodded. "Long hours and low pay, just like being a cop anywhere else, I guess. But yeah, the cases were sometimes very troubling. I was just a patrol officer, but I knew pushers and prostitutes by their first names and could get information on the streets pretty easily. Here, I'm totally out of my element. I don't know if this quaint little town even has a seedy underbelly."

"I'm sure every town does," Hamilton said. "They're just proportionally smaller in places like Apalach. So, what is it I can help you with?"

"I know this will sound like an odd question and I wouldn't want to cause you to break any confidences, but I'd really like to see Apalachicola's ugly side first-hand, so I'm looking for someone who knows the people and how the game's played here."

"First, we just call it Apalach here," Hamilton said. "You mark yourself as a tourist calling it by the full name. Second, as I said, it's a small town. It sounds to me like you want to visit the trailer park over in East Point and need a confidential informant to show you around?"

"One trailer park?" Charity asked. "That's the whole bad part of Apalachic...er...Apalach?"

"The nearest," she replied. "There are a few other hot spots scattered across the county. Let me ask you something. How long ago were you a cop?"

"Not long after Sydney," Charity replied. "I did a couple of years in the Army after 9/11, flying helicopters, then joined Miami-Dade PD for three years. In 2006, I moved over to Homeland Security."

"Homeland Security?"

"I worked with a counterterrorism unit in South Florida, Lieutenant."

"Please just call me Maggie, okay?"

"If you'll call me Charity instead of Ms. Styles."

"So, it's been sixteen years since you were a cop?" Maggie asked. "Things have changed a lot, Charity."

"How so?"

"For one thing, there doesn't have to be a bad part of town or a seedy underside. These days, with instant communication and the Internet, crimes—especially drug-related—take place nearly as often in upscale, gated communities as they do on the other side of the tracks."

"Do you know someone in town, or nearby, who is... shall we say, in touch with the criminal element?"

Maggie thought about her request for a moment, which stretched into several seconds. Finally, she put her cup down and tented her fingers over it. "I might know someone," she replied.

"We're a little too close to discuss any such matters between the two of us, so maybe someone from the outside, someone like you, might be able to learn something from him."

"I promise to share anything I learn."

"Will you be around town for a while? I'll need to call him and get the okay."

Charity looked at her watch. "My laundry won't be finished for at least an hour or two."

"Take a walk over to Battery Park," Maggie said. "If he agrees, I'll ask him to meet you there in one hour. If he says no, he just won't be there. He's very punctual."

CHAPTER FIFTEEN

At the appointed time, Charity again parked her car on the Bay Avenue side of Battery Park Marina. She got out and looked across the fairway toward the boat ramp. Rivera and his friend, Kenny, were gone, as was their little boat. She put on a large pair of blue-tinted sunglasses as she gazed toward Jojo's boat. She didn't see anyone there, either.

A light wind at her back pushed strands of hair ahead of her and tugged at her blouse as she crossed the street and entered the well manicured little park area.

Near a playground, two young mothers were watching over a trio of toddlers at play in a huge sandbox. A group of young people, old enough to be out of high school, leaned against a car, as if waiting for someone.

Not seeing anyone else around, she decided to make herself visible and took a seat on a bench facing south toward the marina and the large bay just beyond. The sun was nearly at its zenith, and she tilted her head up, closed her eyes, and enjoyed the warmth of the sun on her face and the wind in her hair as she considered what she'd learned so far.

Why am I so interested in Jojo and his whereabouts?

He wasn't the only small, Hispanic-looking man around. And the fact that he drove an expensive black car wouldn't convict him. If he *had* been the person who sold the oxy to Karin Bishop and her friends, Rivera would have had a reaction when she'd mentioned his name. The kid had practically bared his soul with his eyes and mannerisms.

When she opened her eyes, a man was seated cross-legged next to her on the bench. Not right beside her, but a couple of feet away. She hadn't seen him as she entered the park and hadn't heard him approach. He was in his fifties, maybe early sixties, fit-looking and well-dressed, with crisp, tan linen slacks and a green, long-sleeved cotton shirt. His light-brown hair was buffeted slightly in the gentle wind.

"Hello," he said, turning to look at her.

He wasn't what Charity had been expecting. She wanted to learn more about crime in the area, particularly about prescription drug abuse and who was selling it, not the latest stock trends. This man looked more like a retired businessman. Or a retirement community player.

"I'm meeting someone," she said to the man, expecting that he was macking her.

He smiled and scratched thoughtfully at his right eyebrow with his index finger. The mannerism seemed engrained, a part of who and what the man was.

"I know, Miss Styles," the stranger said softly. "Maggie asked if I could come down here to talk with you."

A couple of teenagers approached on the sidewalk, wandering in the direction of the others waiting in the parking lot. When they looked over at Charity and the man seated beside her, they exchanged whispers and quickened their pace.

"You're the confidential informant?" she asked.

He looked out over the water for a moment, then slowly shook his head downward, as if amused. "I think my daughter gave you the wrong impression of me."

"Your dau—" Charity started to say, then studied his face again. The hair color was different, but there were enough similar features to lend credence to what he'd claimed.

"Maggie's mother was destined to marry another man," he said, continuing to gaze toward the bay. "Grey raised Maggie as if she were his own daughter and I didn't interfere. But that's not what you wanted to talk to me about, was it?"

"I'm new in Apalach," Charity said.

When she started to explain, he cut her off. "Not that new. You've been here over six months." He pointed to the end of the dock. "Your boat, *Wind Dancer*, was docked right there for the first several weeks and now you're anchored on the lee side of St. George Island near the airport" —he turned and looked her in the eye— "where you keep, of all things, a vintage, Vietnam-era helicopter."

Charity hoped her expression didn't give away the shock she felt at the sudden realization that a stranger knew that much about her.

"You use Rudy Haverstock's pier now," he continued, speaking softly, as he again looked out over the water. He didn't appear to be secretive; it seemed more like his normal speech pattern—calm and quiet. "You go to and from your boat there, parking your car in the Haverstocks' driveway." He paused and looked at her again. "You spend far too much time alone on your boat for such a beautiful woman."

Charity actually felt her face flush. Here was a man who wasn't on the make, but simply stating his opinion. She was incredulous at his boldness, yet deeply flattered at the same time.

"You've been watching me?" she asked bluntly, as was her nature.

He smiled and fixed her with piercing blue eyes, as the breeze lifted a tuft of his hair up off his forehead. "I know everything that goes on in Apalach."

"I'm not sure I like that," Charity said, a bit leery of the man.

"Maggie said you're a PI and you're looking into the deaths of two young people."

"That's right," Charity said, nodding slowly. "She told me she knew

113

someone I could talk to who would know something about crime in the area and the players involved. She offered someone she was too close to, someone she herself couldn't use as a confidential informant."

His lips parted in a half-smile. "She did, eh?"

If this man was Maggie Hamilton's father, and if he actually knew things about criminal activity in this part of the state, as well as the people involved, it was certainly understandable that Hamilton wouldn't go to him herself. Or maybe he was actively involved in criminal activity.

"Do you know anything at all about drug smuggling in the area?" she asked him, point-blank. "Specifically, prescription opioids like oxycodone?"

"You don't beat around the bush, do you?"

"Beating bushes doesn't flush out a wary adversary," Charity said.

He pushed his thick, brown hair off his forehead and stared out over the water again. "You will undoubtedly do some research when we part," he finally said. "And from that, you will understand why I stayed out of Maggie's life. The fact that I'm the biological father of the sheriff's top investigator has sort of become public knowledge around here in the last couple of years. My name is Bennett Boudreaux. I own several businesses and properties from the Big Bend to New Orleans. And yes, I know a good deal about other criminals in the area."

"Other criminals?" she asked.

He turned and faced her again, his eyes boring into hers. They were clear and bright, and he had the beginnings of tiny crows'-feet at the corners—laugh lines. But his eyes also revealed something else, something dangerous.

"Some would say I've...skirted the law," he conceded. "But I've never been convicted of any crime."

"Charged?"

"A few times," he replied openly, then looked back out over the marina. "Your boat? It's different from all these plastic toys. May I ask what make it is?"

"*Wind Dancer* was built before the advent of production-line boats," Charity replied. "She has no *make*. She was hand built in a family-owned shipyard in New England in 1932, from a John Alden design."

"The marine architect who designed some of the fastest sailboats of the early twentieth century?"

"I'm impressed," she said.

He turned to face her again and his eyes went cold. "The man you're looking for is from Pensacola. His name is Antoine Nucci. But you're wasting your time."

"How so?" she asked. "Do you think I can't find him?"

Boudreaux stood and faced her, the sun directly behind his head, making it impossible for her to make out his features well. "I've no doubt you can find anyone you set your sights on, Miss Styles, whether they're hiding out on a volcano in Mexico, way up the Orinoco River, or on some yacht in the Caribbean. But by the time you find Nucci, he'll likely be floating face down in the bay."

Charity's senses went on full alert. She looked up at Boudreaux as he made his cold announcement. She could hear the gulls laughing out on the end of the fishing pier, the children playing make-believe behind her, the soft rustle of sable palm fronds to her right.

"You should get back to your boat soon, Miss Styles," he advised, looking up at the clear blue sky over the trees. "It will start raining in less than an hour."

Before Charity could say anything, he turned and walked away, leaving her with a feeling of panic, something else she was very unaccustomed to. How could he possibly know anything at all about her past assignments? Only a small handful of people knew where she'd been over the past several years.

She slowly exhaled, not realizing she'd been holding her breath.

The gaggle of teenagers who'd been in the parking lot had moved to the shade of a live oak. As Boudreaux approached, they immediately moved out of his way. Several yards out of his way.

CHAPTER SIXTEEN

Charity drove slowly across the bridge, heading out of Apalach. Before leaving the park, she'd used her phone to search the Internet, snooping into Bennett Boudreaux's background.

Publicly, he was prominent, but not ostensibly so. No personal bio on a corporate website, no social media, nothing more than listings of his holdings along the Gulf Coast and a few news stories where he seemed to be on the periphery of a number of police investigations.

How did he know anything *about me?* she wondered, as she drove across the bridge. The Internet held no clues about the places he'd mentioned she'd been. And if he knew where she'd been, did he know what she'd done? And what of her comings and goings here in Apalach?

She could understand a wealthy, prominent man having people all over town doing his watching and intelligence-gathering for him. Or was it something of a more personal nature? He was at least ten years her senior—probably closer to twenty. Charity had no illusions about powerful men of that generation. Many used their wealth and power to attract much younger women.

Perhaps some informant had told him about a new woman in town, just keeping track of the comings and goings that might be of interest to a businessman or crime boss or whatever Bennett Boudreaux was. And then, perhaps, he'd had them do more checking, purely out of personal interest in an attractive woman, new in town. But how could they find out about Mexico and Venezuela, or more importantly, *Heart and Soul?* The other actions had been in other countries. But the yacht had been in San Juan, Puerto Rico, a territory of the United States.

Charity Styles wasn't shy about her physical appearance and knew she possessed the kind of looks that turned men's heads. She often used that to her advantage. Or she used to.

There was something in Boudreaux's eyes that warned Charity to watch out for him. She sensed that he was a very dangerous man. Not in a physical way. He was slight and attractive, with well-manicured hands that didn't look like they'd done a day of labor. Not the hands of the typical head-busting type.

His threat lay in the power and allegiance his wealth brought. Power over the people around him. People who would gladly do his bidding to stay in his good graces.

Stopping at the little laundromat, Charity picked up her clothes, all neatly folded inside the freshly washed laundry bag. She tipped the young woman working there and got back into her car.

How did Bennett Boudreaux know about her helicopter? That was perhaps the most troubling part about meeting him. All the other stuff was related to things and places in the past. The helo tied her to that past life, the life that he'd somehow found out about. But it also pinpointed her in current time. If an ordinary person could learn of her past, Armstrong Research, with all its connections and technology, could easily find her location.

Very few people at the airport knew her chopper was there, and only two of those knew her by name. Pilots and the operations that supported them were a tight-lipped bunch of people.

She'd flown the bird only twice since bringing it up from the Caymans, so odds were someone on the mainland had seen her come or go and maybe they had a good friend who worked at the small airfield.

Boudreaux didn't look the part of a crime boss, but what did one look like these days? Maggie had been right; Charity hadn't been a cop in a long time.

During her time with DHS and later with the CIA, and then Armstrong, her assignments had all been abroad, with the exception of *Heart and Soul*. Still, what she did at Armstrong wasn't all that dissimilar to being a real private investigator. Just in different parts of the world. She'd observed, asked questions, and even used her wiles for information.

"Isn't that what a PI does?" she asked aloud, the wind carrying her words away as she drove across the long causeway to St. George Island.

As she sat stopped in the right turn lane for Bay Shore, the shadow of a cloud passed over and it began to rain. She quickly reached back between the seats to pull the convertible top's release, and the roof popped up. The car behind her honked, but she ignored them as she pulled the top up into place and latched it.

Three seconds after the first raindrop hit her thigh, she eased the clutch out and made the turn, shifting up through the gears.

People were always in such a hurry, she thought, looking in her rearview mirror. God forbid you might lose two seconds out of your precious day so someone else could avoid being drenched.

She switched the wipers and headlights on as the rain began to fall harder. She'd checked her weather app before leaving that morning and there had been no mention of rain.

But Boudreaux had predicted it.

She'd met a few people who'd seemed to be able to sense approaching storms. A friend of Jesse's by the name of Rusty Thurman, whose lineage in the Florida Keys went back many generations, always seemed to know when severe weather was coming.

Finally, she turned into the Haverstocks' driveway to find Jojo's car also parked there. The rain showed no sign of letting up, but Charity was prepared. Opening the console storage, she pulled a plastic garbage bag from a small box and opened it, then placed her shoes on top of her laundry bag and pulled the trash bag over it so the plastic bag was upside down covering everything.

She'd get wet, as would the clothes she was wearing, but being wet was second nature to Charity. She opened the door and stepped out into the deluge, hurrying along the path around the side of the house and out onto the dock.

She ran in bare feet all the way to the covered gazebo at the end where her dinghy was tied, holding the bag to her left side with both arms around it. The rain pelted the metal roof as she set her bag on a bench and slung her hair from side to side, flinging water out of it. The white blouse clung to her skin, outlining her form; she wasn't even wearing her usual bathing suit top under it.

Peering through the sheets of rain out across the bay, she saw gray clouds stretching to the horizon. She glanced back at Rudy and Heather's house, but the windows were dark, except for the upstairs. She looked down at her body and decided she didn't want to appear at their door like that, especially with Jojo and The Buddha also likely to be there.

"I can't get any wetter," she said to herself, as she pulled the dinghy up to the ladder and climbed down.

Reaching up, she grabbed her laundry bag and put it under the seat where at least her clothes would stay dry. It wasn't the first time she'd been caught in an unexpected rainstorm, and probably wouldn't be the last.

She started the little outboard and untied the line, then was quickly up on plane and headed toward her boat. Not as fast as she'd like to go, but as fast as the stinging rain against her practically bare flesh would allow.

As she got nearer and angled for the starboard side, she noticed a paddleboard tied to the stern cleat. She stopped the dinghy instantly and put the outboard in neutral.

Her left hand went to the hem of her skirt, which was difficult to pull up due to her being seated and it being sopping wet. Then she saw Jojo stand up in *Wind Dancer's* cockpit.

"Are you okay?" he called out, cupping his hands.

"Son of a bitch," she muttered, as she put the outboard back in gear and surged quickly toward the boarding ladder.

She lashed the painter to a rail post and climbed quickly up to the side deck, flinging the sunshade up and dropping down into the cockpit.

"What're you doing on my boat?" Charity demanded, her voice loud and firm.

"I—I apologize," Jojo stammered, staring at her. "I was out for a paddle and got caught in the..." He turned slightly away from her, casting his eyes downward. "I'm sorry. You should get out of your wet clothes before you get a chill."

Charity felt a chill, all right. And it had nothing to do with the weather or being soaked to the bone. The number one cardinal sin among boaters was boarding without permission.

Charity looked down at her fists, clenched in rage, her lungs heaving as adrenaline coursed through her system. The white blouse was no longer white. At best it was semi-translucent, having been plastered to her by the wind and spray from the speeding dinghy. She looked like some co-ed at a frat house wet T-shirt contest.

In an instant, the rage was gone, replaced with remorse at having spoken to the kind and gentle little man in such a harsh way. He wasn't the drug dealer she'd suspected him of being. He was just a businessman.

"I'm sorry, Jojo," she offered, turning to unlock the companionway hatch. "That was uncalled for. Please wait here for just a minute, okay?"

Charity went down the steps and quickly moved forward to her stateroom, where, for the first time in a long time, she closed the door to change out of her wet clothes.

She pulled her blouse out and unbuttoned it, then flung open the hanging locker, suddenly realizing her clean clothes were still in the dinghy. The hanging locker was empty.

After closing the locker, she opened the drawer beneath it, already knowing what she was going to find. One lime-green bikini, a second white one, and a red one-piece, along with a floral beach wrap she'd picked up in St. Thomas.

"Crap," she muttered, then turned and opened the door partway. "Jojo, are you still out there?"

"Yes," he replied, his voice meek and subdued.

"Could you get my laundry bag from under the dinghy's seat, please?"

She heard him cross the deck and then the squeak of the boarding ladder against the hull as he climbed down. A moment later, he appeared at the companionway hatch.

"Everything seems dry," he called down.

"Would you mind bringing me the bag?" Charity asked, feeling wicked for putting the mild-mannered man in such a state. "Those are the only clean clothes I have."

He came through the salon quickly but hesitantly, a man unsure of himself or uncertain about the situation he'd found himself in.

Charity opened the door enough to take the bag from him. As she started to close it, his eyes came up from the deck and for an instant, he could see her blouse hanging open and her wet hair dripping water down her torso.

She latched the door as the adrenaline coursing through her body slowly started to subside. The rush had brought up other thoughts and feelings. As she peeled off her blouse and wiggled her hips to get her skirt down, she wondered what the man might be like in bed. For a moment she entertained the idea of flinging the door open, wearing nothing but the DB9 in its holster, still strapped to the inside of her thigh.

That would be cruel, she decided, then quickly unstrapped the gun, shoved it under her pillow, and pulled on a pair of cargo shorts and a favorite T-shirt instead.

Opening the door, Charity stepped out of her stateroom. Jojo stood in the middle of the salon, staring through a starboard porthole as the rain pelted the cabin top.

"It doesn't look as if it's going to let up any time soon," she said.

"I am very sorry," he said sheepishly. "I wanted only refuge from the storm, but when you didn't answer my calls, I should have continued on to the pier."

There was a flash of lightning, awfully close by, followed almost instantly by the loud boom of thunder. Jojo jumped slightly.

"Don't be silly," she said, taking a step toward him. "You might have been struck if you hadn't stopped here."

He turned and looked at her a moment. "Still, I had no permission to board your boat. It is an act of piracy."

"Yaarrgghh," Charity growled, making the man smile.

CHAPTER SEVENTEEN

Borrowing his neighbor's moped, because the battery in his dad's truck was dead, Lucas Rivera rode across the bridge to East Point. He almost wiped out when he spotted the blonde's blue convertible parked at the laundromat. He turned his head, hoping he'd catch a glimpse of her again, and the moped veered off the road.

Once he managed to get control and steer the little motorbike back into his lane, he continued through the small town on US-98, and just before Gulf Coast Auto, he turned onto David Street, winding the little engine up as he headed toward the bay.

Approaching the stop sign across from Bayshore Trailer Park, he could see through the trees that there was nothing coming from either direction, so he barely slowed down.

When Lucas pulled up to the third trailer on the left, he parked next to Leo Bishop's Mustang and killed the engine, spotting Leo on the porch.

"What're you doin' here?" Leo asked, rising unsteadily from a chair in the shade of an awning.

A bottle of cheap rum sat on a table next to Leo's chair.

Lucas got off the moped and pocketed the key. "I need to talk to you, man."

"About what?"

"Not out here," Lucas said, moving past him. "Let's go inside."

The inside of Leo's trailer was a mess. It was always in disarray, but now it smelled, too. At least he was alone.

Leo came up the steps behind him. "What the hell you doin' bargin' into my crib?"

"We need to find that Antoine guy," Lucas said, turning to face him in the shabby living room. "The guy Karin had bring the oxy out to us last week."

Leo flopped down on the couch. "Oxy's easy to find," he said. "Hell, I got three left."

"Lemme see."

"I ain't gonna let you *see* shit, man," he slurred. "You here to buy or what?"

"The shit Karin got last week wasn't what we usually get," Lucas said, pulling a straight-backed wooden chair closer to the makeshift table in front of the couch and sitting in it. "It was like, extra-strength or something."

"Whatta *you* know, man? You told me you'd only tried it a few times."

"A PI came to see me," Lucas replied. "She told me about the oxy and damn near killed Kenny."

"Huh?" Leo grunted, then started laughing. He took another swig from the bottle, then wiped his mouth with the back of his hand. "A private dick who's a chick? What'd she do to Kenny?"

"Knocked his ass out with a single punch to the forehead, man. I've never seen anything like it. And she had a gun. It was in a holster up under her dress."

Leo grinned again. "No way, man! That's friggin' cool."

"Look, bro, I'm real sorry about what happened and all. I liked your sister a lot." Lucas paused and waited for Leo to look at him. "We gotta find this guy who sold us that potent stuff, man. He's the reason she's dead."

Leo sat up a little, placing the rum bottle on the table. "How you know those pills were stronger? Tell me what the private eye said."

Lucas recounted the story, leaving out the part about how turned on he'd been about the hot older blonde. He realized now that she'd intentionally let him look up her skirt for just that reason, to throw him off-balance. And it had worked.

"One punch?" Leo asked.

"Yeah, and her knuckles were bleeding from it. Kenny just collapsed in the boat, man. He was out cold for ten minutes. Then she licked the blood off her knuckle! Like that chick Angelina whatever in the movie."

"How'd she get there?" Leo asked.

"The marina?"

"No, dumbass!" Leo lashed out. "Fucking Pluto!"

Lucas knew he was drunk—probably high, too. He was trying to drown the pain of losing his sister. He'd been messed up before, but now it seemed like his mood swings were about to go over the top.

"She drives a blue sports car," Lucas said. "Looks like one of those Miatas."

"Think she's working with the cops?"

"I dunno, man," Lucas replied, shaking his head. "I don't think they share a whole lot."

"You mean on TV they don't," Leo scoffed. "Ever met a real PI before? Talked to them about how they work? And what was that shit about the Jojo dude?"

"I think that's the real reason she came to the marina," Lucas said, thinking back. "She was looking for him, then it seemed like she suddenly recognized me, and knew the lady cop had just left."

He regretted saying it as soon as the words left his mouth.

"The sheriff's old lady?" Leo asked. "What the fuck did she want?"

"*Former* sheriff," Lucas corrected him, then paused. "I got something to tell you about that. That night, I mean."

Leo sat forward. "What?"

Lucas looked out the window at the side of the trailer next door. Rain began to pelt the roof, splashing back up in the air. He could hear it on Leo's roof, as well. He looked over at him and hung his head a moment.

"I was with her, man," Lucas said without looking up.

"Who?"

"I was with Karin that night, man."

"Duh," Leo said mockingly. "Everyone knows that. So was half the football team before she even quit school. What's your point?"

Lucas looked up, feeling a tinge of resentment. "No, man. I mean I was with her when she died."

Leo looked at him, the haze of the rum lifting slightly. "We were all there, bruh. She died in the back of your truck while we were partying."

Lucas slowly shook his head. "I was in the back of the truck with her, man."

"You what?" Leo shouted, starting to rise, but stumbling back into the cushions.

"I'm sorry, man!" Lucas exclaimed. "I freaked out, okay?" He hung his head again and wiped the back of his hand across his eyes. "I've never seen anyone die before."

"You mean you knew she was dead and was just whoopin' it up with the rest of us?"

"It wasn't like that, man. Honest!"

Leo managed to get to his feet and nearly stumbled over the small table. "Wasn't like what, man? You tellin' me you left my sister dead in the back of your truck for half the fuckin' night and didn't tell anyone?"

Lucas stood and faced his friend, vigorously rubbing his face with both hands before pulling his hair back to the top of his head.

"I was *with* her when she died, man!" Lucas shouted, his face a mask of anguish.

The realization of what Lucas had said seemed to get through the alcohol fog and he lunged at Lucas, swinging wildly with a closed fist. He missed and almost went down, stumbling over the table.

"You think I wanted to tell you that?" Lucas yelled.

Leo's mouth fell open as he sat back down hard.

"She took two of those pills," Lucas said, his voice breaking as he remembered the details of that night. "She said she'd done two before, but we didn't know the ones we bought were like double the usual dose. One would be enough to knock out a big man."

Leo slung his fist into the cushion next to him. "I *knew* it was a better buzz than I usually got and it hit me as soon as I took it."

"They're called 'immediate release' and they kick in almost as soon as you swallow them."

Leo pointed toward the kitchen. "In there, man. Second drawer beside the stove."

Lucas walked over and opened the drawer. In the back was a small plastic sandwich bag with several pills. He pulled it out, unrolled it, took one of the pills in his hand, and looked at it. It was blank, except for a depressed line which would make it easier to cut in half. Moving his thumb, he turned the tablet over. The number 10 was engraved into the other side, along with the letters IR below it.

He carried the bag back to the living room.

"See?" Lucas said, handing the pill to Leo. "The ten means milligrams. Twenty will kill you if it's this immediate-release shit. That's what the IR stands for."

"Fuck me," Leo sighed, looking at the tablet in his hand. "That guy should have said something."

"No shit," Lucas agreed. "We gotta let everyone know, in case someone else still has a stash."

Leo looked up at him as thunder rolled in from the bay. His eyes were red and moist. "And we gotta find the son of a bitch who sold them to us. He killed my sister."

CHAPTER EIGHTEEN

Charity and Jojo spent half an hour sitting in the salon, talking about random things as the rain drummed steadily on the cabin top. Nothing more was said about his trespassing or her near nakedness when confronting him. Mostly they talked about growing up in SoCal, and as it turned out they'd had a few favorite places in common.

The rain suddenly stopped, and their voices sounded unusually loud in the confined silence. The storm had given them reason to be there. The outside world was nothing but the rain and the water. Beyond that was everything else, but it wasn't in contact with them. It'd been as if they'd been wrapped together in a cocoon and the rain stopping had been the signal that the silky threads were parting.

"I should be going," Jojo said. "My friends are probably worried."

"You didn't call to tell them you were out here?"

"I forgot to bring my phone," he replied. "I usually carry it in a dry bag. They were on the dock when it started raining, so they saw me stop here."

He rose and moved toward the companionway. Charity, who was closer, got there first, unlatched the little half doors, and slid the top hatch open. She climbed quickly up the steps and looked around.

The storm and its tall, anvil-headed clouds had moved off to the southeast, leaving behind a solid gray, overcast sky. The sun was trying to break through the thinner cloud cover to the west, but not making much headway.

"The lightning is way off and moving away," Charity said, turning to face Jojo as he came up the steps. "I can take you back in the dinghy, if you'd like."

"Thank you, no," Jojo said. "You have been very hospitable, and as you said, the storm has passed."

They said goodbye and Jojo stepped down the ladder onto his board, quickly positioning his feet to stand. "Will I see you again before we leave?" he asked, looking up at her.

"That's very possible," she replied.

"I would like that," he said, then dipped his paddle.

She watched for a moment as he paddled toward Rudy and Heather's dock, then looked toward the west. The sun was there, hidden by the gray cloud bank. She checked her watch. It was nearly eight o'clock and the clouds weren't going to part enough for her to see the sunset.

After descending back down into the salon, Charity headed forward and opened her laptop at the navigation station. She connected to the Haverstocks' Wi-Fi to do a deeper dive into Boudreaux's background and see what she could find out about Antoine Nucci.

Her search proved nearly fruitless with Boudreaux. She did come across an old news story about his saving a woman named Maggie Redmond from being swept away in flood waters during a hurricane. The story said she was an investigator for the Franklin County Sheriff's Office.

Maggie must have gotten married since then, Charity thought. After she confirmed that Maggie Redmond and Margaret Hamilton were the same person, she used just her new last name along with Apalachicola, and several newspaper accounts of Maggie's investigations over the past several years appeared. Then, on page three of the results, down near the bottom, she found the headline, *Sheriff Wyatt Hamilton Resigns.* The picture matched the tall man Charity had seen Maggie with coming out of Boss Oyster.

She wondered if their getting married had anything to do with his resignation. The story didn't go into much detail.

Her search for the name of the man Boudreaux had given her resulted in several arrest reports in local papers from Pensacola and the surrounding area going back several years, but nothing in Franklin County. Most of his arrests were on drug-related charges, but there were two burglary charges from nearly ten years ago, and one assault with a deadly weapon charge. That one should have landed him in prison for a long time, but the charge had been dropped due to a technicality.

Reading between the lines, Charity figured the local cops in the spring break capital of the South had screwed up the investigation.

She found several pictures, mugshots mostly, and from his Facebook page, she saw that he spent a lot of time at strip clubs in the area. Further digging revealed he was the owner of one of the clubs. She added the address to notes she kept on her phone.

Darkness fell both outside and over the kind of information she was digging up as she worked at her laptop for over an hour.

"Smut and drugs," Charity whispered aloud, closing the computer. "I wouldn't be too sure you get to him first, Mr. Bennett Boudreaux."

Charity didn't care for men like Antoine Nucci. No, that was putting it mildly. She despised them. The more she found out about him, the more she wanted to put her hands around the man's neck and squeeze the life out of him while kicking him repeatedly in the groin until she collapsed from exhaustion and he was as swollen as grapefruits. But even that was too good.

She found herself being sucked in again. She knew it wasn't going to be enough to just let Mr. Conti know the name of the man who'd supplied the drugs that killed his friend's son.

The smart thing for Charity to do would be to forget her helo and car, hoist anchor and just sail away. She had enough money to last her several lifetimes and buy a fleet of cars and helicopters. The inlet leading to the open Gulf of Mexico was just a short sail to the east. Once out in the Gulf, she could turn west and head for New Orleans or the Texas coast, maybe even Mexico.

Thinking about what Boudreaux knew about her and realizing that Armstrong, or one of her many enemies, might be able to find her just as easily, Charity suddenly remembered something.

"*Whole Nine Yards!*" she whispered softly, her head jerking toward the open hatch.

Reaching up to the electrical panel, she flipped off the twelve-volt breaker for the cabin lights, pitching the boat's interior into shadowy darkness.

DJ Martin had a boat by that name.

As she moved quickly to her stateroom and pulled the DB9 from under the pillow, shedding the holster and dropping it on the bed, she mentally kicked herself for not checking the boat's home port below the name.

Could it have been the same boat that was tied up in front of Jojo's? Was Martin here looking for her? Why him? She liked the guy and got the vibe that the feeling was mutual. Surely, he'd turn down any assignment to come after her and bring her back.

Slowly exposing her head in the companionway, she looked all around the boat. There was nothing there. She put the gun in her pocket, then closed and locked the hatch.

Returning to the nav station, Charity turned on the spreader-mounted motion detectors, setting them on maximum sensitivity to alert her if anything moved within a hundred feet of her boat.

Next, she switched on the radar and set it on low power mode and short range, covering only that part of Apalachicola Bay between her boat and the mainland to the north. It would emit an audible alarm whenever a boat moved past on the ICW, but hopefully they'd be few and far between.

Satisfied that nobody could get close without her knowing it, she went to her stateroom and raised the bunk. From a secret compartment, she took out a cheap cell phone, one of a dozen she'd picked up at stores all around the area, paying cash for each.

After punching in a number she knew by heart, she waited.

"Hello," a woman's Southern-accented voice answered.

"Chyrel, it's me."

There was a rustling sound and then footsteps. A door opened and closed, then Chyrel spoke. "Charity?"

"Yeah. Hey look, I need to ask you something and if you can't answer honestly, just don't answer at all, okay?"

"What do you need to know?" Chyrel asked.

"Is DJ Martin on an assignment?"

Chyrel's reply was quick. "DJ? No, he told Jerry he was going for a sail three weeks ago and just disappeared. He called Mr. Stockwell a week later and told him he'd be unavailable for the rest of the summer. Nobody knows where he is."

Charity thought for a moment. Chyrel was a former CIA computer analyst and they'd worked together with Homeland

135

Security. CIA people were very adept at keeping secrets, but Charity was sure her friend wouldn't lie to her. After all, she was the one who'd made it possible for Charity to disappear.

"He took *Whole Nine Yards* for a sail and just never came back?" Charity asked, dropping in DJ's boat's name. "That sounds out of character even, for him."

"I'm not sure if he took *his* sailboat," Chyrel said. "Or if he chartered one. I do know his sport fisher is in Bimini. I was there last week and saw it, but I didn't think to ask if he'd sailed in his own boat, or what."

"And *you* don't even have a way to track him?"

"All his electronic assets are turned off," Chyrel replied. "What's going on?"

"DJ's here in Apalachicola."

"Oh," Chyrel said softly.

"Is there something you're not telling me?" Charity asked, suddenly concerned.

"He might know where you are."

CHAPTER NINETEEN

Charity woke before the first hint of daybreak, her decision made. Before leaving *Wind Dancer*, she ate a protein bar and put a banana in the pocket of her hoodie for later. If there was to be a confrontation, she was going to initiate it, and she wasted no time in getting ready.

After what Chyrel had told her the night before, she felt almost certain that if Martin was in Apalachicola, it was by chance. She'd said that she'd been talking to Jesse one day about six weeks ago, when she'd gone to Bimini, and he'd asked confidentially if she knew where Charity was and what she was up to. Charity trusted Jesse completely and didn't have any problem with Chyrel telling him that she was in the Florida Panhandle.

But Chyrel suspected that Martin might have overheard them, as he'd appeared at Jesse's office doorway a moment later.

Charity barely knew DJ Martin, but she knew the sort of background he had. Besides being one of Armstrong Research's undercover operatives, Martin was a former spec-ops soldier—a staff sergeant if she remembered correctly. He'd lost a leg in Iraq to an IED.

She didn't want to hurt the guy, but she wasn't going to let anyone from her past find her first.

Rather than go to the Haverstocks' house and drive over into town, Charity decided to take her dinghy across Apalachicola Bay. It would get her there faster, even at just over planing speed, and it would keep Martin from knowing her car. And cars were pretty limited forms of egress if she had to get out fast.

She'd decide what to do about DJ Martin after seeing the man.

Dressed in dark pants and the hoodie, Charity climbed down into her RHIB and started the outboard. Looking around, she got her bearings, spotting the line of lighted channel markers in the ICW and the glow on the northern horizon that would be Apalachicola.

With her head only a few feet above sea level, anything beyond two miles was over the horizon and the distance to town was twice that.

Crossing a navigable waterway the size of Apalachicola Bay in a small dinghy was ill-advised, except in good conditions. Darkness added even more danger. And her dinghy had no lights. But the little boat was quick and maneuverable and there weren't any sandbars or shallows to worry about.

She untied the painter and settled onto the back bench seat where it was attached to the starboard pontoon. Pointing the bow toward town, she put the little outboard in gear and twisted the throttle until the little boat began to plane out.

The water was as flat as any inland pond, and she pushed her speed up a little more. The only real danger would be encountering another boat, but the channel was clearly marked, and she saw nothing else in sight.

It had been a new moon just four days earlier, and the waxing crescent wouldn't rise until about half an hour after the sun. So, all she had to guide her were the stars and the glow on the horizon, which quickly became individual lights as she got closer.

Once she crossed the ICW, she could distinguish the marker lights for the channel leading straight toward the marina where she was sure DJ Martin was asleep on his boat.

It took less than twenty minutes for Charity to reach the entrance to Battery Park Marina. She didn't see another boat the whole way and the marina entrance was clear. So, she slowed the dinghy and stayed well to the left as she idled in. With her hood pulled up over her head. She could see the upper part of Martin's boat just around the dogleg. It was still in the end spot and Jojo's boat was right behind it. Both were dark.

She made the turn, staying close to the boats on her left, and once past *Bottom Line II*, the Haverstocks' Hylas, she angled toward the boat ramp. Killing the engine while still fifteen feet away, she allowed her boat to drift as she stood and surveyed the area. There wasn't a soul in sight and no traffic on the streets.

When the dinghy reached the dock, Charity quickly tied it off and stepped up. Pulling her hood back to her forehead for better visibility, she looked all around. She'd been wrong—DJ's boat wasn't completely dark. A slight red glow emanated from the cockpit.

She moved toward it, feeling the weight of the holstered DB9 on her hip under the sweatshirt. It was a comforting feeling. As she got closer, she realized the red light came from two small LED fixtures mounted close to the deck. They shined downward, effectively illuminating where a person would be walking if anyone was up and about. The fact that they were on gave Charity pause.

Was he up already? Or had he just forgotten to turn them off? Small LEDs didn't draw a lot of power, so maybe he'd intentionally left them on all night.

Slowly, she stalked past *Bottom Line*, raising the tail of her hoodie to expose the handgun. With her hand resting on the grip, she slipped past *Arva* and approached *Whole Nine Yard's* cockpit. When she glanced down at the transom, she saw the boat's home port was Key Biscayne.

It was definitely Martin's boat.

An upturned bucket sat next to the boat's cockpit—a makeshift boarding step. Charity picked it up quietly and moved it beside the dock's electrical pedestal, which his boat was plugged into, then sat on it and waited. From her vantage point, she could see the cockpit, as well as the length of the dock stretching to where her dinghy was tied. Turning her head slightly, she could see the rest of the dock around the dogleg, all the way to the end and out into the bay. She was close enough to the pedestal to be almost invisible in the darkness, and it blocked anyone seeing her from inside.

After sitting there for twenty minutes, with the sky to the east just starting to turn purple, she heard a soft tweeting sound coming from inside the boat.

Whole Nine Yards moved slightly, and the sound stopped.

An alarm clock, she figured.

The boat settled and became still once more. Charity couldn't hear any movement from anyone inside. Seconds ticked by and became minutes.

Then the tweeting started again. This time, the boat moved even more, and she heard a grunting sound as the alarm's snooze button was turned off.

An inconsistent thumping sound came from inside, moving aft, and a light came on in the rear part of the salon. She heard cabinets being opened and closed, and then the sound of running water.

Everything became quiet for several minutes, then Charity smelled coffee. The boat moved again, and the thumping continued to the companionway hatch. The hatch slid open, and a hand reached out, placing a mug of steaming coffee on the deck.

Charity realized what the heavy thumping was when Martin hopped up the steps, pulling himself up with his arms. He wasn't wearing his prosthetic.

"Lose your pegleg?" Charity asked.

Martin suddenly rolled forward onto the deck, clawing at his pocket as he came up in a modified kneeling position.

Charity already had her gun out and leveled at him. "Uh-uh. Don't even think about it."

DJ's hand moved slowly away from his side, where Charity was sure he had a weapon. "Who the hell are you?" he asked, his voice somewhere between a snarl and a shout, low enough so as not to wake anyone on other boats.

"Real slow," Charity said, masking her voice a little. "Using just your thumb and forefinger, take the weapon out and toss it down below."

Martin did what he was told, knowing he was helpless to do anything else. When he tossed the gun, it didn't clatter across the deck but instead, Charity heard a soft whoosh. He'd managed to toss it onto a seat or cushion.

Charity pulled her hood back, stood, and dropped the DB9 to the low ready position, both hands still on the grip and ready to bring the gun to bear in a second.

Martin's eyes went wide. "Charity?" he said, his voice hushed. "What the hell are you doing here?"

"I might ask you the same question."

"Come aboard," he said. "And for Christ's sake, put the friggin' gun away."

"Did Stockwell send you to look for me?" she asked, making no move to board his boat or holster her weapon.

"Stockwell?" Martin looked confused. "Why would—? Wait. You think I'm here to *hurt* you?"

"Who sent you?"

"Nobody *sent* me, Charity," he replied. "I'm not here after you or anybody else."

"Why *are* you here?"

"Can I get up?"

"Over on the starboard bench," Charity said, motioning with her gun as she stepped closer to the boat's gunwale.

Using mostly his arms and upper body, Martin made it to his foot, then slid onto the bench. "I'm just passing through," he said. "Not on my way to or from anywhere."

"What's that supposed to mean?"

"I got no idea, man," Martin said, shaking his head. "I just started thinking about where I was going and what I was doing. So, I decided to go for a sail. You know, just to clear my head. A week out of Key Biscayne, I found myself anchored off Cedar Key, up north of Tampa, and saw the most gorgeous sunset I think I've ever seen. But I couldn't even point it out to someone and say, 'Hey, ain't that pretty?'"

Charity relaxed her posture a little, lowering the gun to her right thigh, in case anyone were to come out and see her standing there. "So, you just went for a sail?"

"Yeah," he replied, leaning back, and draping an arm over the edge of the seat. "Travis isn't there, by the way."

"Travis Stockwell?"

He grinned. "Travis McGee. Jimmy Buffett said he was still in Cedar Key. He ain't. I looked all over."

Charity wasn't a huge fan, but she'd heard the trop-rocker's songs and knew the one he was talking about.

"Why'd you take off?" she asked, genuinely curious.

"I don't know," he replied. "I hooked up with the Armstrong network to find my way. Now I'm thinking my way isn't their way."

"And Jerry Snyder?"

"Dep? Oh, I'm sure he's glad to be rid of me. Um, can I reach over and get my coffee?"

Before he could move his arm, Charity vaulted the gunwale, picked up the mug with her left hand, and placed it on the small table between them. Then she sat down opposite Martin, keeping the gun on her lap.

"Thanks," he said, taking a sip and looking over his mug at her.

He absently reached down just below the stump of his right leg, then sat back with an expression that seemed born of complete frustration.

"What's wrong?" she asked.

"You mean besides gettin' the shit scared out of me first thing in the morning by a pretty lady?"

She nodded toward his stump. "You seem a little more frustrated than usual."

"Phantom itch," he said. "Drives me nuts sometimes. Especially wearing the leg."

"A phantom itch?"

"You ever have to wear a cast?" he asked.

She nodded. "From my elbow to my wrist."

"Remember how you'd get an itch, but couldn't scratch it?"

She nodded again.

"I get one on the outside of an Achilles tendon that hasn't been attached to my body for fourteen years." He looked at her for a moment, his expression neutral. "Seriously. You can put the gun away. I ain't gonna hurt you."

"That statement presumes that you *could* hurt me."

He cocked his head a little and grinned through what looked like a month of beard growth. "Oh, I think I could hold my own."

"In a wrestling match, yeah," Charity countered. "You're obviously stronger. Maybe even in a stand-up brawl with your pegleg on, but anything that took more than ten seconds, I'd be all over you."

His grin broadened to a smile. She remembered she'd liked DJ Martin's smile.

"Ya know," he said, "that might be an interesting proposition."

Charity huffed in exasperation, then placed her pistol on the seat beside her. She leaned on her elbows, staring into Martin's eyes. "When was the last time you talked to anyone at Armstrong?"

His gaze never wavered. "Almost two weeks ago. I called the colonel on a burn phone and told him I wouldn't be available until fall."

"What'd he say to that?"

"Ya got me," he replied with an amused shrug. "I dropped the phone in the drink."

"I threw my company phone overboard several months ago," she said without thinking.

"When I said *in the drink*, I didn't mean overboard. I called him from a dive bar in South Beach, during a period of rum-induced lucidity. I'd decided then and there to change my life. After I told him he wouldn't hear from me for a coupla months, I dropped the phone in my drink. I've been sober ever since."

Charity saw no indication that he was lying, and his statement matched what Chyrel had told her. Except the sobriety part. For some reason, it pleased her. She was happy for him.

"So, why Apalachicola?"

He shrugged. "It's about halfway between Cedar Key and Pensacola. And it sticks right out into the Gulf, so it's either stop at it or go around it." He took another sip of his coffee. "What're *you* doing here? Besides scaring the shit outta sleepy sailors, that is."

"Right now, I'm looking for a drug dealer."

CHAPTER TWENTY

Over coffee, Charity laid out for DJ most of what she'd learned so far, deciding that his being there was at least not at AR's behest. She left out some of the details concerning her meeting with Jojo the previous evening.

"I'll go with you," DJ said when she finished.

"Go where with me?"

"You're goin' to P'cola—same as me. And you want to find this Nucci guy before Boudreaux does, right?"

"So?"

"Have you ever taken a good long look at yourself in a mirror?" DJ asked. "First street hustler you talk to will make you for anything *but* a pill head."

"I didn't know all drug users looked alike."

"They don't," DJ replied. "But most opioid users *are* lazy. And lazy means lard-asses. You're just too fit to pass yourself off as an oxy user."

"I have my ways," Charity said, maybe a bit too crossly. "It's not like I'll be prowling the streets in a bikini, trying to find this guy."

"No offense," he countered. "I'm sure you could probably pull it off with the right clothes, mussed up hair, and some makeup so you don't appear so glowingly healthy. But I'd bet your hanging locker and drawers don't contain a single article of clothing with a tear or hole. Ratty clothes I have plenty of. I have the natural looks to be able to buy drugs from any dealer."

He had a point. "You looked the part of a druggy a lot more before that big party in San Juan when you shaved and put on that tux."

"Hey, you missed out on all the excitement!" DJ said. "By the time we got back to the yacht that night, rounded up all the bad guys, and found Eisenstein dead in his shower, you were long gone."

"Yes," Charity said. "I had to leave suddenly. A few days later, I got the goods on Snyder's friend, Arlen Burkhart."

"I don't think they're what you'd call *friends*," DJ said.

"I watched him kill a man."

"No way!" he practically shouted. "Jerry could use that!"

"I thought you didn't care about Deputy Do-right."

"Yeah, well... Who was it?"

"Never saw him before," she replied. "Burkhart called him Mr. Edwards."

DJ thought for a moment and shrugged. "No bell ringin' there." He eyed her curiously across the tiny salon's dinette. "The other bartender from the aft lounge was gone too. When Dep checked with the boat's skipper, he said everything about both of you had been erased from the yacht management company's computer." DJ made a poof gesture with both hands. "Like you were never there."

"I wasn't," Charity said, crossing over to refill her mug from the pot. "That bartender was a woman named Christy, I believe."

"Uh-huh," DJ said, nodding slowly.

"The other bartender was underage," she said, looking out a starboard porthole at the boats lining the other side of the fairway. "Probably best for the yacht management company that they lost her records."

"Word leaked out," DJ said to Charity's back. "Rumor has it that Eisenstein died doing some sort of erotic auto-asphyxiation thing."

"I wouldn't know anything about it."

He stared at her a moment. "No," he finally said, drawing the word out. "I'm sure you wouldn't. So, whatta ya say? Want me to tag along? I'm a fair sailor and even better navigator."

"How are you at reading a road map?" Charity asked.

"Better than the average Army officer," he said with a grin. "You have land transport here?"

"Land, sea, or air," she replied.

"Now you're soundin' like Captain McDermitt."

Charity laughed. She and Jesse McDermitt went way back. She knew him as one of the kindest and gentlest men she'd ever met. Sure, he had a violent side, as did Charity, but that part of his DNA was always laser-focused. To people he cared about, he was a giant teddy-bear.

"Yeah, I have a car," she said, sitting back down. "It's kind of small and not much leg room."

"I can always put one leg in the backseat," he said with a grin.

"Not in my car," she countered. "It doesn't have one."

"Ooh, Jane Bond!" he said with a chuckle.

"Get your phone."

"Can I take a minute and put my leg on, too?" he asked. "I can get around a lot better with it."

"Yeah, but we're not leaving immediately. I just want to send you a couple of photos."

He used the overhead hand holds, swinging his way forward like a chimp. Inwardly Charity smiled remembering how he'd entertained the little girl on *Heart and Soul.*

149

"Hey, whatever happened to that little girl?" she asked. "Was it Flor?"

"Yeah," DJ replied, opening his hanging locker, and flipping through his wardrobe. "I talked to her a coupla weeks ago. She's doin' a whole lot better now. She was so happy that her hair was growing back."

The little V-berth in the bow of the boat was open to the salon, with nothing more than a curtain separating the two, which was pulled back, revealing his prosthetic leg lying on the deck beside the bed.

"What should I wear?" he asked as he pushed and shoved to get the artificial lower leg over his stump. Then he pulled the sleeve up over his knee and buckled it. "It's a college town, right? Maybe a polo shirt and jeans?"

"It's a spring break town and spring break is over. The part of town we're going to will probably be a little on the seedy side."

"Four-twenty casual, then," he said, unbuttoning his long-sleeved denim shirt.

She'd never seen DJ bare-chested before. When he shrugged out of his shirt, it was obvious that he'd lost most of the pudginess he'd carried around the middle, now replaced with a decent set of abs.

But it was his upper body that drew Charity's attention. With only one leg, he likely had to use his arms for a lot of things most people took for granted, like getting up off the deck. His chest was well-sculpted—slabs of muscle rising up to broad shoulders and bulging arms.

He pulled on an oversized, tie-dyed Grateful Dead sweatshirt that'd seen better days. It had the caricature of the *Truckin'* man in the center, leaning back, and taking a big step. Somehow, the shirt made him look soft and overweight again. Or maybe her perception was the result of knowing him as he was before.

"How'd you get back in shape so fast?" Charity asked.

"Three weeks of eating only what I could catch," he replied, adjusting the shirt so it hung loosely. "Did I mention I'm a much better sailor than I am a fisherman?"

Charity laughed as he sat back down across from her.

"I turn forty in two months," he admitted. "This ain't a mid-life crisis or anything, me just up and leaving like I did. I seriously needed to rethink my whole life and I think I've gotten at least a few things straightened out."

"So, why are you so hellbent on helping me?"

DJ finished his coffee and set the mug down. "One—I think you need the help. And B—I'm bored to death here."

"One and B, huh?"

"I don't always think in what most folks would call a straight line," he offered with a shrug. "Sometimes, that's a good thing."

"No, really," Charity said, putting her own mug beside his. "I'm perfectly capable of taking care of myself—I've worked solo for a long time. Bringing closure to these kids' families by putting Nucci behind bars won't be much of a challenge after some of the things I've done."

DJ looked down at his hands, absently rubbing at new callouses, likely born from line-handling. Solo sailing wasn't easy. Unless you had power winches like *Wind Dancer's*.

Finally, he looked up at her, his eyes saddened. "I used to have a big sister," he said. "She died of a heroin overdose."

CHAPTER TWENTY-ONE

After weeks of high-energy partying two months earlier, with thousands of young people flocking to the beaches, shops, and bars in March, Pensacola was downright boring through the hot, miserable summer. Memorial Day weekend was less than four weeks away, the start of the summer season for normally sleepy little tourist towns. Then, the spark would ignite once more. Not with the same unabashed exuberance that fanned the flames of the college crowds, but with a crush of people just the same.

It was the spring breakers that kept Antoine going. The thousands of college students who descended on the town were all seeking the same thing—escape and fun. It was two weeks of unbridled alcohol- and drug-induced inhibition.

Antoine had made a boatload of cash in March. Enough to float him through the rest of the year. But he wanted more. He always had. By making an occasional run through the small Gulf Coast towns, selling product in bulk at separate locations, he was slowly building a network. What he made selling prescription drugs to locals all year long paled in comparison to his spring break haul. But that was how associations were built. And Pensacola wasn't the only spring break hot spot.

Sure, there were other locals already in place who got pissed when he sold to their customers. But that'd only happened after they'd refused to do business with him. Antoine's name and attitude opened a lot of doors.

"Why we still hangin' out here?" Eli asked.

Eli Harris was Antoine's top runner. He had a way of ingratiating himself into the groups of young people and easily outsold his other runners. He also never got caught, which was every bit as important as moving product.

There were four of them. His runners' jobs were just that. They ran back and forth, moving small amounts at a time and returning with cash. That way, if they *did* get caught by the cops, they weren't carrying much of either, and were usually released the next day.

Antoine knew none of his runners would ever *fare la spia.* The penalty for narcing was high in *La Famiglia.* Not that Antoine was a part of the mob or anything—he'd never even met a real *mafioso* before—but he never corrected those who assumed his connection, and even went as far as to drop an occasional reference to being a part of it.

Antoine looked over at the slightly built, sandy-blond-haired high school dropout. "There's no rush to leave, *amico mio.*"

Though he *was* of Italian descent, Antoine Nucci was born in Florida, as were his mother and father. Neither of his parents spoke much of their traditional language, but Antoine peppered his speech with Italian words and phrases and had even perfected the accent.

"We could go to 'Nawlins," Eli said, his Louisiana roots evident in his speech. "Plenty a room to expand dere. And I know people."

"You don't have any trouble making friends anywhere," Antoine countered.

"It's the accent," Eli offered. "Everbody loves a coon-ass."

ELUSIVE CHARITY

He was partly right. Eli wasn't a big man and looked a lot younger than his thirty-one years. So, the young college guys didn't feel threatened by him, and as soon as he opened his mouth the women seemed to melt at his feet. He was a fun-loving guy on the outside, ready to help visiting revelers in their quest to escape. He had a knack for making everyone around him feel comfortable and for gaining their trust.

"We're good until Memorial Day weekend," Antoine said. "Everyone needs time off. But we do need to go on another collection run. Did you get the scripts?"

Eli nodded. "Yeah, but my guy at the VA said next time it's gonna cost more."

"We're already paying him ten bucks a copy. What's he want?"

"Fifteen," Eli replied. "Says it's way more dangerous for him dan me, taking de time to scan each doc's prescription."

"Tell him okay," Antoine said, though he didn't like it. "But also tell him no more of this five-and-ten pill shit. I'll pay his fifteen bucks. But only for scripts over fifty pills. Otherwise, he can just fuck off and go pound sand up his ass. People like that are replaceable."

The two men sat at a sidewalk café in the mid-morning heat. It had a drive-thru in the back and a small living space above. Antoine was drinking a strong Italian espresso, and Eli, just a regular coffee. The café was in Seville Square, a short walk from Old Town or to the beach.

There was only one other occupied table, and it was on the other side of the patio. A middle-aged businessman, his suit coat hanging over the chair next to him, was showing a much younger woman a stack of papers, flipping through them, and quietly pointing out things written there. Occasionally, she signed one of the pages.

The two had arrived separately, the woman on foot, and though she'd seemed tense when she'd arrived, the man's mannerisms and soothing tone—though Antoine couldn't hear what either was saying—seemed to be making her more relaxed.

Probably a divorce lawyer, Antoine thought, having considered the two at great length while he waited for Eli.

He'd heard somewhere that divorces in the area went up right after spring break. Especially among younger couples. It seemed the influx of young people brought out infidelity in the locals.

"When do we make the collection?" Eli asked.

"Too late in the week to start now," he replied. "We could only hit a couple dozen pharmacies before Sunday. Let's meet here Monday morning."

"Den I tink I might go up to Shreveport," Eli said. "Haven't seen my little brother in over a year. Want me to take a couple dozen scripts with me? We ain't done nothin' dere before."

"That's not a bad idea," Antoine said, as the woman at the other table laughed at something the man said, then looked at him in disbelief.

Antoine couldn't hear her words, but it was evident she'd responded with, "That much?"

"Take twenty with you and have them filled at twenty different pharmacies there," Antoine said, watching the woman. "Then Monday, we can drive over to Tallahassee and work our way back."

She had long, chestnut-colored hair, an elegant clip holding it in place at the back of her neck, where it hung down to the middle of her back. She looked to be about the same age as Antoine and the tan line on her left ring finger was as white as the man's hair— evidence she'd been married for a while but recently separated.

In Florida, marital property was split fifty-fifty unless the property was acquired prior to the marriage. If a couple married young and had nothing, then became successful with only one of them having an income, the non-working spouse would get half if they divorced.

Eli finished his coffee, set the paper cup down, and glanced over at the woman with the older man. When he looked back at his boss, Antoine was grinning lecherously.

"Monday then," Eli said, then got up and walked away.

Antoine caught the waitress's eye and lifted his small cup. She nodded and went to the window. A moment later she returned, smiling, and placed another espresso in front of Antoine, scooping up the empties.

"I don't know how you stay so calm and cool in this heat drinking that," the waitress quipped.

He smiled up at her and lowered his sunglasses slightly. "I am *Italiano*. It is what we do."

He'd seen the young blonde many times, and knew she was struggling to make ends meet. All the previous year, he'd seen her occasionally at clubs, always with a man several years older. But lately he hadn't been in the picture.

Antoine had heard that she'd ended what her friends had called a toxic relationship and was currently staying in a small, one-bedroom apartment above her café and waiting tables to avoid hiring another server.

"Um, just out of curiosity," he said, motioning her to lean closer, her back to the other table, "do you know that guy over there and the woman he's with?"

"I don't know his *name*," she said. "But he's a lawyer. The woman is a good friend of mine."

"It is a game I play," Antoine said with an innocent-looking smile on his face. "Trying to guess random people's occupations. I had him pegged as a lawyer but wasn't sure about her. A banker?"

"Close," the waitress said with a smile. "She's a secretary for a group of stockbrokers."

"That would have been my second guess," he said. "Do you know her well? Why is she seeing a lawyer?"

The waitress looked over her shoulder then back at Antoine.

He smiled innocently. "As I said, it is only a game."

"She's getting a divorce," she replied.

"That is sad," he said with a frown.

He lifted his small cup in salute, and she turned with a flourish, sauntering back to the shade of the partially open interior in a way she was sure he'd notice.

Antoine pushed his shades back up and grinned. "I do love it here," he said softly.

The café was only a few blocks from the house where Antoine had grown up and now lived alone. His parents had given it to him when they'd divorced ten years earlier, though both had left the house and the marriage long before they'd officially dissolved the partnership and moved to different parts of the state.

His parents both had someone else in their lives for some time before they left. In the last few years of their marriage, each had often taken long business trips separately. His mother now lived in Orlando with her boyfriend, and his father had moved up to Atlanta and remarried within a month. Antoine liked Pensacola and had decided to stay. He'd only been eighteen at the time, just out of high school.

The waitress walked back out as Antoine finished his espresso. She took the man at the other table his credit card and receipt, then came toward Antoine. The man signed the receipt, put his card away, straightened the papers the attractive brunette had signed, and put them in his briefcase.

"Anything else?" the waitress asked with a bright smile.

Antoine smiled back. "Yes, Layla. I was thinking of going for a walk on the beach this evening before sunset. Maybe you'd like to join me and then perhaps we could hit a few clubs after?"

Her smile brightened. "That sounds cool! I get off at four."

The brunette rose, shook the silver-haired man's hand, and started walking down the sidewalk toward the middle of town. Behind his dark sunglasses, Antoine's eyes followed her hips.

"I'll be back then," he said as he stood, pulled two twenties from a roll in his pocket and placed them on the table.

"I'll see you at four, *la mia amante*," Antoine said, then turned and walked toward his home, following ten yards behind the brunette.

"Time to play," he whispered as he walked with a lewd smile on his face. Unbeknownst to her, the secretary was about to have the time of her life.

CHAPTER TWENTY-TWO

"This your idea of fun?" DJ shouted from the passenger seat as the Spider hugged another curve.

As flat as Florida was, it still had its share of winding roads, and once out of Apalachicola and neighboring Port St. Joe, US-98 was no exception.

When DJ had offered to help, Charity returned to her boat, grabbed a go-bag with essentials, stuffed another with clothes, and had then driven back to the marina to pick him up.

"I thought you Screaming Eagles were all high speed and low drag," Charity replied, raising her voice over the wind and road noise.

"If I wanted high speed in my middle years, I'd have stayed aboard *Ambrosia*."

The boat he'd mentioned was the current pride of Armstrong Research's fleet of vessels. But *Ambrosia* was a research vessel in name only. There *were* technicians and sophisticated oceanographic research equipment onboard, even a submersible, but its primary function was as a mobile command center. And with a top speed of sixty knots, she was very mobile.

Once through the small town of Mexico Beach, the two-lane highway ran straight through the palmetto- and pine-covered landscape for as far as the eye could see, disappearing into the distance.

Charity eased up on the throttle slightly, the speedometer dropping to seventy-five miles per hour. The tach wasn't anywhere near yellow.

"What made you decide to buy a car?" DJ asked. "Especially a race car?"

Charity smiled, glancing over at him through large, dark-tinted sunglasses. "This isn't a race car."

"Maybe not in the pure sense of the word," he allowed. "Yeah, it's got A/C, a radio, and cruise control, but it's still a race car. How fast will it go?"

"The manufacturer says one forty-four," she replied. "But I've never had it over one-thirty."

"Why the hell would you wanna go that fast in a convertible?"

"Wait till you've been cruising a few more years," she replied. "Don't get me wrong. I love *Wind Dancer*—that's my boat—but fifteen years at six knots can become tedious."

She downshifted and hit the gas, moving into the oncoming lane as they came up behind a slower car. There was a moment of turbo lag, then g-forces pushed them both back into their seats as the little car accelerated. Once clear, she shifted back into high gear and eased up on the pedal. But not a lot—the speedometer now hovered at a little over eighty.

DJ looked down at his phone. "Better slow down. We're coming up on Tyndal, then a sharp right, and into Panama City."

Charity backed off, noting the reduced speed limit sign as they approached the home of the Air Force's 325th Fighter Wing. She knew how hard military police could be on civilians passing through or around their installations.

"You ever talk to a psychologist about that phantom itch?" Charity asked, as buildings began to spring up on the right.

"A shrink? What the hell for?"

"Don't play stupid, DJ. You know full well that your foot doesn't itch. It's in your head."

"My great-aunt told me once how her second husband had one—a phantom itch on a finger he'd cut off with a chop saw. He'd buried it in the backyard and she'd told him to go dig it up and straighten it."

"Oh, that's just gross!" Charity said. "Why would he even bury it in the first place?"

"Dunno," DJ said with a shrug. "But Aunt Sal told me when he dug it up and straightened it out, he never had the itch again."

The two rode in silence as the number of buildings—a random mixture of hangars, offices, barracks, and workshops—became more densely packed.

"What did they do with your—?"

"Cremated, incinerated, and dumped in a land fill," DJ replied, as if expecting the question.

"Cremated and incinerated?"

He shrugged. "Cremated at the field hospital and sent to the dump where all garbage is incinerated before going into the fill."

"I suppose digging it up and straightening it is pretty much out of the question then."

DJ looked over at her and laughed in a mocking way, slapping at his knee. "You're actually kinda funny when you let yourself go."

"I'm sorry," she said.

"Don't be. That's always been Dep's biggest hang up. He couldn't see me for the prosthetic. You seem to be able to ignore it."

"I'm sure it's limiting," Charity offered. "Any advantages?"

"Not on the deck of a boat, I can promise ya that. But going up the mast in a bosun's chair is a breeze. I weigh about twenty pounds less than a guy with a comparable build."

"Well, there's that," she said, smiling over at him as she downshifted for the long, sweeping curve coming out of Tyndal. "I'll give you a call next time my spinnaker halyard gets stuck."

After a few more miles, DJ looked over and asked, "So, are you like, seeing anyone?"

She glanced over for a couple of seconds, then returned her eyes to the road. "Seeing anyone?"

"You know...like dating?"

She laughed, then called to mind a couple of men she had loved, both dead now. "Seriously? In our line of work?"

"I was just curious," DJ said.

Several more miles slipped past as they entered Panama City.

"I'm single," Charity said. "Like your leg, it's a permanent affliction."

"I didn't mean to dredge up anything painful," he said, as if reading her expression.

"I've had a few relationships," she said, her voice cold. "They died."

"I'm sor—"

"Don't you dare say that," she snapped. "After we finish this up, it'd probably be best for you if you sailed on."

"Yeah," he said, turning forward again. "Sure thing."

As Charity was about to say something, he glanced down at his phone. "After this left curve coming up, hang a right on Transmitter Road. Stay on that for two-and-a-half miles, then turn right on US-231."

Most of the single men Charity had met always seemed to be on the make. They couldn't spend ten minutes alone with an attractive woman without trying to get her out of her clothes.

As she turned onto the side road, she glanced over at him again. He was being intentionally silent. She shifted up through the gears, maintaining the legal speed.

She recalled the sight of DJ playing with the sick girl and glanced over at him again, pretending to check her mirror. He hadn't had any ulterior motive trying to make the girl smile.

Maybe he was different from the others.

After she turned onto the U.S. highway, DJ checked his phone again.

"Another two-and-a-half-miles, then left on 77A."

"Are you going to be like this the rest of the trip?"

"Like what?"

Charity sighed, frustrated by his typical male reluctance to express his thoughts and feelings. "I don't do relationships well, DJ," she said. "I never have. My mom left when I was little, Dad died when I was a teen, and I just never let anyone get close for a long time. Then I did. He was killed in a bomb blast meant for Jesse and Deuce."

"Deuce Livingston?"

"Yeah," Charity said. "By a former DHS deputy director—a man named Jason Smith. He went rogue, tried to kill the two of them and almost killed the president. This was about fifteen years ago. He tried a second time and a man named Jared, who I'd become involved with, drove off with the bomb meant for them and everyone else who was there."

"You and Jared were close?"

She didn't answer immediately, remembering his face. "We might have been," she finally said. "He was killed instantly in the blast."

"When did you say this was?" DJ asked.

"It was just after I joined DHS."

"You've known those guys that long?"

"Jared was the son of one of Jesse's friends," Charity said. "He was a Marine who'd been wrongfully discharged thanks to Jason Smith. Jesse fixed it so he could reenlist, which he did just before he was killed."

"And this Smith guy?"

Charity glanced over, locking eyes with him. "I broke his fucking neck with my bare hands." She returned her attention to the road as DJ stared at her profile. "Jesse McDermitt was there. Now you and he are the only two who know what happened."

"I had no idea you'd been doing this for so long," DJ said. "I feel like such a wimp for feeling burned out after just a few years."

She looked over at him again. "This is the third time I've done what you're doing."

"Quit?"

"You won't," she said with finality, then let out a sigh. "Nor will I."

CHAPTER TWENTY-THREE

When they reached the interstate, Charity covered the seventy miles to the Pensacola exit in well under an hour. During that time, they'd put together a rudimentary plan to locate Nucci, both knowing any sort of elaborate plan would just be a waste of time. Reality rarely remained consistent with a plan. One person's reaction might be different than expected and would set in motion a whole new set of actions and reactions from others. They were going to pretend to be a couple looking for a fun time. Beyond that, they'd play it by ear.

First, they'd have to find a hotel near where their quarry might be located. They already knew he owned a strip club, and there were five more nearby, most on or near US-29 and I-110, the main roads into town.

DJ did some more digging into the man's social media, locating pictures with landmarks in the background. He was able to determine where a few of them were located using image search. Nucci seemed to spend a good deal of time in the old Seville Historic District.

"His club's only a mile from where I think he either lives or spends a lot of his time," DJ said, as Charity drove slowly south into the heart of Pensacola.

"Find a hotel near his club," Charity suggested.

"One room or two," he asked, as his thumbs danced on the phone's tiny keypad.

"We're pretending to be a couple," she replied. "And before you ask, two beds."

"Wasn't gonna ask," he said, his head down to block the sun's glare on the screen.

"Oh?"

He glanced over and grinned. "Variety's a good thing."

"Not gonna happen, DJ."

"Okay, I found two," he said, ignoring her and looking back down at his phone. "A Holiday Inn not far from his club, or a little boutique hotel in Seville Square, overlooking Pensacola Bay. That one's really expensive."

"Book us a room at the boutique hotel," Charity said.

He stabbed the phone's screen a couple more times, then laid the phone in his lap. "Do you really think we can find this guy? I mean, what if he's pushing pills over in Apalach this week? Or somewhere else?"

"You said yourself—he posts on social media quite a lot but there are gaps where he doesn't post anything for several days. Those are likely the days he's out in the field, so to speak. When was his last Facebook post?"

DJ tapped at his screen and scrolled a bit. "Just a couple of hours ago, from a coffee shop in Seville Square."

"There you go," Charity said, downshifting and turning off on the last exit.

"Stay in the middle lane for Chase Drive, headed west," DJ said, checking his map app again. "As soon as you merge onto Chase, get in the left lane and turn onto Tarragona Street."

A few minutes later, Charity steered her Spider under a small portico at a quaint little hotel, then continued through, spotting a parking spot close by. DJ got out and Charity quickly raised the roof and climbed out on her side. They grabbed their bags from the small trunk and went inside.

Once they'd checked in, they took the elevator to the top floor and found their room. It overlooked the water and from the balcony, they could see most of the waterfront.

"This is perfect," Charity said, stepping back into the room.

"Yeah," DJ replied, pulling a holstered Kimber 1911 from his pack, and clipping it to his belt. "Now all we gotta do is find one guy out of about fifty thousand people."

Charity placed her laptop on the desk and opened it. "One in twenty-five thousand," she corrected him. "Only half the population is male."

"And how do you plan to do that?" he asked. "Just sit on the balcony and wait for him to walk by?"

"It'll be easier if we let him find us," Charity said. "We know he lives here in Pensacola—even Boudreaux said that—and we're fairly sure he lives in this part of town. So what was he doing at an abandoned farm out in the middle of nowhere a hundred miles from here?"

"Abandoned farm?"

"Something Lucas Rivera told me," she replied. "Karin Bishop—the girl who overdosed more than a week ago—had told Rivera she could get a guy named Antoine to deliver a hundred oxy tablets, and this guy, who drove an expensive-looking black car, had then delivered the drugs right to the party site."

"So, he's not a street hustler but more of a distributor," DJ said, nodding his understanding.

"A distributor," Charity agreed. "But I don't think an excessively big one, or even all that smart. Most of the upper echelon criminals I've encountered didn't use social media at all."

"Like that Boudreaux guy you were telling me about?"

"Exactly," Charity said. "The more I think about it and the more I learn about him, I'm convinced he's one of the top dogs in the criminal world around here."

"Like the way you said those teenagers looked at him," DJ said. "Kids are a lot more in touch with that element. I used to have a buddy who trafficked a little here and there. The older he got, the less acceptable he was to both the younger people he dealt with and the criminal population as a whole. It's not easy for a user or street hustler to trust anyone over thirty."

"And unlike Boudreaux, Nucci seems to have a lot of presence on the Internet and in social media."

"Makes sense," DJ agreed, pacing the room. "Being a criminal isn't difficult. Being successful at it means you have to be smart."

Charity nodded. "And Nucci is no Boudreaux."

"You think his threat carries any weight?"

"Yeah, I do," she replied, going back to the laptop. "It's not just what he said—that was clear enough—but more about his body language and the look in his eyes. The man has some seriously scary eyes. And then in a microsecond, they change to soft and romantic."

"You mean like yours."

She turned and glared at him.

"See, you just did it," DJ said. "You were thinking about how cuddly the guy was and your eyes were all smoky and warm. And now they're tossing daggers at me."

She turned back to the computer, embarrassed that she'd let the guy get under her skin. Both guys.

170

"Smoky and warm?" she asked, without looking up.

"Describing what you see in a person's eyes isn't easy," DJ said. "I saw something in yours that afternoon on that yacht, when I caught you scoping out the helicopter."

She couldn't deny that she'd found him charming...in a way. Charity had always been attracted to tall, rugged-looking men. A girl's first love is usually her father and many grow up to be attracted to men who are similar to him, either in appearance, manner, or both.

Charity's dad had been well over six feet tall and powerfully built; a big man, especially from the perspective of a smallish girl. His face had been tanned from long hours in the sun, with deep lines across his forehead and at the corners of his eyes and mouth. He'd almost always had a stubble of beard on his face. A lot like the men she'd been attracted to over the years. Men like Jesse, Jared, and Victor.

And DJ Martin?

"So, we just put the word out that we're buying?" DJ asked, thankfully changing the subject.

"It's a start," she said. "It's too early to hit the bars looking for him, and we both missed lunch. How about an early dinner?"

"I can always eat," he replied.

"Did you notice a particular restaurant Nucci seemed to frequent?"

"Google Images is pretty good at identifying landmarks," DJ replied. "Not so much with restaurant interiors. But he does eat out a lot and seems to prefer Italian."

"What about that coffee shop?" she asked, removing her holstered DB9 and clipping it to her belt under her blouse. "The one he was at earlier. It was outside. Do they serve food?"

Charity saw him admiring her handgun. Or maybe it was the flash of skin to which his eyes had been drawn.

"His post was actually a check-in," he said. "So, I know exactly where it is. It's only a few blocks from here." He pointed to her holstered sidearm. "That's a cool-looking piece. I don't think I've ever seen a pea-shooter that small."

Charity pulled her pistol from its holster, dropped the magazine into her left hand, and racked the slide back, ejecting the chambered round onto the bed. Then she turned it and handed it to him, butt first.

"It's a DB9 model, made by Diamondback Firearms. Chambered for 9mm, it's hardly a peashooter, though less than an inch wide."

DJ took the gun and examined it, then gripped it in both hands, assuming a shooting stance, with the barrel pointed out the sliding door.

"It's really skinny," he noted.

"Looks even more so in those mitts you call hands," she said. "I needed something slim to be able to ship it. I have a special makeup case with false side panels concealing a one-inch hiding space, enough room to hold two of those with four loaded mags. I can ship or carry that case just about anywhere and it never gets scrutinized."

"What about X-rays?" he asked, handing the gun back.

"The hidden compartment has a thin lead shield," she replied, reloading, and holstering her gun. "Same as the other three sides. In imaging, it just looks like rounded and reinforced edges. With a jumble of small items in the case like nail polish, eye liner, hair dye—it's all very distracting, and pulls prying eyes away from the sides."

"Sweet," he offered. "How many rounds does that thing hold?"

"Six more than I would normally need," she replied, opening her small suitcase.

"Uh-huh."

She stopped removing her clothes and looked up at him. "What's that supposed to mean?"

"Nothing," he said vaguely.

"Spit it out, DJ."

"Well...we've never, um...worked together," he started slowly. Then he looked up and locked eyes with her. "All I know about you is that you were a medevac pilot and worked for DHS."

"Between the two, I was a sworn officer with the Miami-Dade Police Department," she said, getting a little irritated. "I was a martial arts instructor there and qualified expert with a handgun."

He held her gaze. "I'm more interested in the part of your life before we all hooked up with Armstrong. Going back to the theft of an aircraft assigned to Homeland Security down in Homestead."

Charity took a deep breath. "Anything associated with that was removed everywhere," she said. "Permanently."

"I know," DJ said. "It's the why that concerns me. I looked everywhere there's a record of you. You and that helicopter just disappeared for a really long time. Not even a civilian paper trail."

"I was loosely attached to the CIA."

"Yeah, you told me that," he said. "Chyrel was with the CIA and sat behind a desk."

Charity sat down heavily on the bed and motioned him to sit on the opposite one. When he did, she took a deep breath. "What I'm about to tell you, only two other people in the world know—Colonel Stockwell and Jesse McDermitt. Deuce may have an idea; Jesse might have told him some of it to keep him from digging."

"Some of what?"

She took another breath and let it out slowly. "For several years, I worked as a covert operative."

"And?"

She fixed him with a steady gaze. "I was an assassin, DJ. I worked as an assassin for the CIA."

He only stared at her for a moment, as if digesting what she'd told him. "Where?"

"Not in the States," she replied, looking down and picking at a chipped nail. "My first assignment was a terrorist cell that was training in Mexico. My target was the leader of that cell."

"What happened?"

"I killed them all," she said, her voice frosty as she looked up at DJ. "I caused a volcano to erupt, sending every last one of them straight to the fires of Hell."

"Wait...what?" he said. "When was that?"

"It was in the spring of '07."

He was silent for a moment, thinking. Then his eyes focused on hers. "San Martin Tuxtla?"

"How'd you know that?"

"There have only been nine volcanic eruptions in all of Mexico in the last hundred years," he said. "Only three this century—two composites and a shield." He shrugged. "I kinda have a thing about volcanoes."

"A thing?" she asked.

"I climb them," he said, breaking eye contact and looking out the window. "Walk around the craters as close as is allowed."

"Why?"

"I don't know," he said, still staring out at the bay. "Tempting fate, maybe. My first deployment was Iraq. After the invasion. Nights on an active volcano kinda remind me of the fires." He blinked hard and looked back over at her. "So, yeah, I know a little about the subject."

"So you know what a fumerole dome is?" she asked.

"The cooler rock over a vent or fissure that seals the magma in."

"I shot the Tuxtla dome with depleted uranium incendiary rounds," she admitted, remembering how stupid that had been and how close she'd come to incinerating herself. "Four times."

DJ stared at her in disbelief. "You made the volcano erupt," he whispered in amazement.

It was a statement, not a question.

"That was my first mission," she said. "I killed twelve terrorists that day and it was almost my last mission."

"Huh? Why?"

"Aside from the obvious—almost killing myself in the process—I was only supposed to kill the leader, a man called Hussein Seif al Din Asfour."

He only stared at her, dumbfounded.

"The CIA takes a dim view on overkill," she said. "It attracts too much attention."

She paused as she searched DJ's face. He'd been right about describing someone's eyes. She'd seen his eyes flash with anger and grow moist with sadness. Just then, they looked like the eyes of the little girl he'd tried to make smile—innocent and trusting.

She blinked. "Eisenstein didn't kill himself."

CHAPTER TWENTY-FOUR

Admitting to DJ that she'd once been a CIA assassin probably wasn't the wisest thing to do. Telling him about the murder she'd committed on the yacht, anchored in American waters, was beyond the pale.

But he did have a point. In their line of work, they needed to know they could rely on each other and he knew next to nothing about her background or what he could count on her to do in a pinch.

Now they both knew one another's capabilities. And weaknesses.

DJ had been a staff sergeant in the Army, part of the elite 101st Airborne Division. That alone told Charity all she needed to know about what he was capable of. Just to be selected for Airborne meant a soldier stood out among his peers. The school and the training that followed were rigorous. And he'd seen combat.

His disability was an obstacle, but one he seemed to have overcome for the most part. How he might handle himself in a fight, or if they had to move quickly, she had no way of knowing.

They were alike in some ways. They'd both been broken—mentally, emotionally, and physically—then put back together in a form alien to what they were before.

The two walked along Main Street with the afternoon sun on their faces and sunglasses blocking it. Charity's were big and blue, a fashionable pair that matched her navy skirt and blue blouse. DJ's were the thin, wraparound kind, all black with black lenses. He too was dressed nicely, in khaki pants and a white guayabera shirt.

He walked closer to the curb, something Charity always noticed about men she met. The act itself came from the days of horse-drawn carts. Men were bigger and more capable of subduing a skittish horse that went by a couple on foot. Charity needed no such protection. To her, it meant that DJ had probably learned this simple act from his parents. Maybe something he'd observed his dad do and had asked his mom about it.

Charity looked over at him. It was difficult for her to imagine him as a little boy. His gait didn't indicate that he was missing half of his lower right leg, and wearing long khaki trousers, nobody could tell unless they were listening closely. The sound of his fake foot was slightly different.

DJ walked straight and tall, head turning and eyes shifting—not missing anything. She doubted a runaway horse cart would get within a block before he reacted to it.

"There it is," he said, pointing ahead.

It was a two-story brick building, painted white, with balconies on the second floor that overlooked a café with open-air seating. DJ had checked and found that it closed at four o'clock; it was already half past three.

They took a seat at one of the tables and looked around. There were a few people scattered at various tables, mostly two to a table. None of them looked like Antoine Nucci.

A young waitress approached and smiled. "We're closing in half an hour," she said. "My name's Layla. Can I get you something?"

"Is the kitchen still open, Layla?" DJ asked, smiling at the curvy blonde. "We missed lunch and it's too early for dinner."

"We don't really have a kitchen," she replied. "Coffee, fruit, pastries, and cookies."

"You mean like a fruit salad?" Charity asked.

"Yeah," the waitress replied. "Or whole fruit. The pastries are fresh, made less than an hour ago for the work walkers."

"Work walkers?" DJ asked.

"People who walk by on their way to and from work. We get a lot of those."

"I guess a fruit bowl would hold me over," DJ said. "And a coffee, please—black."

"I'll have the same," Charity said.

"Coming right up," Layla said, then turned and walked toward the counter window.

DJ's eyes followed her swaying hips.

"We're supposed to be a couple," Charity hissed. "Stop ogling the waitress."

"I wasn't ogling," he said defensively.

"Did your eyes leave even *one stitch* of clothing on that girl?"

"What can I say?" he replied with a crooked grin. "It was a long sea crossing to get here."

"Speaking of being a couple," she said, keeping her voice low, "we shouldn't use our real names. One of my aliases is Gabriella Ortiz Fleming, but people I get close to call me Gabby."

DJ thought for a minute. "I never really used one. How about Blunt?"

She looked at him, curious. "Blunt?"

He grinned. "That's what my *customers* call me. My real name's Robert Blount."

Charity arched an eyebrow. "Is that a real person?"

179

"Was," DJ replied. "At one time, one of my closest friends. He's dead now, though."

For a moment, Charity saw the sadness in his eyes. Then it disappeared and he grinned once more. "Perfect nickname for a small-time dealer, huh? Bobby the Blunt."

She smiled at him as the waitress returned, carrying a tray. "Blunt it is, then."

"Here you go," Layla said, putting the tray on an adjacent table, then moving their coffees and fruit bowls in front of them, along with neatly wrapped silverware in linen napkins. "I had them add extra blackberries and sliced kiwi," she said. "They're higher in protein and should get you through the rest of the afternoon."

"Thanks, Layla," DJ said.

Charity leaned slightly toward the woman. "Um, we're here on vacation," she said with a tinge of East Tennessee trailer park in her voice. "Me and Blunt was hoping to find somethin' a little better than protein to take the edge off, if you know what I mean."

Layla looked at her for a second, then over at DJ. "Blunt? That's not really your name, is it?"

"Last name," DJ replied. "But yeah, my friends use it as a nickname, on account of how it's pronounced back home. In a lot of places it ain't pronounced like a blunt you smoke, but in East Tennessee, you can bet the farm it is. The name's Bobby Blount, B-L-O-U-N-T, and this is my girlfriend, Gabby Fleming."

Layla looked over her shoulder toward the window, then glanced up and down the street. "Sure, I know someone. He was just here a couple of hours ago. But he'll be back at four to pick me up. We're going clubbing."

"I'd love to see some of the top clubs," Charity squealed. "But maybe tomorrow. It was a long drive, ya know."

"I couldn't guarantee that," Layla said. "This is just the first time Antoine's asked me out."

Without taking her eyes from the girl's, Charity saw DJ's head jerk toward her. "Maybe an hour or two, babe?"

"And what about your leg?" Charity asked. "You only brought the regular one."

Layla looked at her puzzled until DJ pulled up his right pant leg. "My dancin' leg's still at home."

She was aghast at first, then caught the look of mirth in his eyes, and covered her mouth, giggling as her face flushed slightly.

"Maybe Layla and I could cut a rug while you boys talk business?" Charity suggested.

"Oh, I really don't know Antoine that well," Layla said. "But he should be here any minute. Let me ask him first."

"Yeah, sure," Charity replied, smiling warmly. "But we'd only be in your hair for a little while."

She left and DJ leaned in close. "Sometimes you're the windshield. Sometimes you're the bug."

"That was too easy," she whispered back. "Nothing's ever that simple. My guess is there's two Antoines."

"That were both at this café at the same time?"

"It can't be that easy," she insisted. "Drive into town, check into a hotel, go to a café, and bust a drug dealer minutes later?"

"Speaking of," DJ said. "Whatta we do with this guy, if and when we find him? We're not cops."

"I haven't thought that far ahead."

"Better start thinking fast," DJ said looking over her shoulder. "Don't turn around, but Antoine Nucci is walking this way."

CHAPTER TWENTY-FIVE

It had all started simply enough, as these things often did. Times were tough, and for those who pulled a living out of the water, it could often be particularly so. Pollution and a dwindling workforce, combined with over-harvesting, over-reaching regulations, and over-zealous law enforcement, had pushed many simple fishermen to seek other means of making a living—some just as a side hustle and some permanently. For every successful commercial fisherman, there were a thousand failures.

Occasionally, the side hustles meant working outside the law.

Claude Landry once had a debt to pay and no way to produce the money in time. Missing the payment would have meant getting his boat repossessed and putting him out of business. So, he'd taken what work he could find around town, and eventually met the man who directed those who worked outside the law. The money paid for the time spent was a lot more lucrative than washing dishes at a diner.

By trade, Claude was an oysterman, which meant prolonged hours standing in a small boat with long, scissor-like tongs, dredging up oysters by hand. The tongs operated much like a posthole digger, except instead of opposing spades, the tongs had wide rakes used to sift through the sand for oysters. The action of raking—moving the handles apart, lifting sand and oysters, moving the handles together, then doing it again, over, and over, all day long, built strong upper body muscles. And at just a shade under six feet, Claude Landry, though now in his fifties, was a powerful man.

When times got tough, Claude had no trouble finding work that paid under the table. He often moved boxes in the back of his van. Those who didn't bother asking what was in the boxes could make decent money, but he still preferred oystering—at least when the buy was good. But he didn't have any trouble doing things that were illegal. After a while, the movement of boxes included returning with payments. A few times, his trips included making sure that those who were slow to pay or short on the amount learned to be on time in the future. He'd busted a few heads.

Killing someone wasn't new to Claude. But he usually got more out of the job than just the elimination of the two grand debt he currently owed the man. He'd tried to make it on his own many times, and always ended up borrowing at the last minute for one thing or another, then having to work off the debt.

When Boudreaux had made the offer, Claude had balked, but only for a moment. It was a way to stay in the man's good graces, and both Landry and Boudreaux knew he'd do it.

And who knows? he thought. *Might even be a little bonus in it.*

Finding the guy hadn't been all that hard. Hell, all he'd had to do was follow the breadcrumbs the creep left online. He seemed to fancy himself as a big player and a lady's man. It was quickly obvious he was neither.

Claude had arrived in Pensacola at midmorning and found the man at a small coffee shop. He'd parked his nondescript, gray Corolla rental a block away, observing him and another man talking at a table. The hi-def dashcam streamed right to his phone and was zoomed in so he could see the two men's faces.

When he was a kid, Claude had known a deaf girl who lived down the street. At first, he'd learned sign language to impress her. She was a pretty girl but didn't have many friends because she didn't talk like other kids. Having never heard words, the sounds came out a little differently than expected because she'd had to learn to talk by watching how sounds were made.

Lip-reading involved more than just the lips, though. The movement of jaw, tongue, and lips made sounds and words, and a person's expressions often told as much as their mouth. Tammi had taught Claude how to read lips, so he didn't have any trouble figuring out that he had the right guy. They'd talked openly about moving drugs in Mr. Boudreaux's territory.

He'd watched the second man leave, then saw Nucci ask the waitress for a date, and she'd agreed to let him pick her up that afternoon. A few minutes later, he'd settled his bill and asked about another couple sitting at a nearby table, saying it was a game he played. After the waitress told him what he wanted to know, he got up to leave, following the brunette who was on foot.

Claude had allowed them to get a couple of blocks ahead, Nucci walking faster to catch the woman. Then he followed them at normal speed, parking on the side of the street once more just a short distance behind them.

He had planned to wait until the guy was alone, then just pull up next to him, and put a bullet in his brain. He could be back in East Point before dark. But he knew that was out the window for the moment as his target caught up to the woman and began talking to her.

She was a looker, full hips encased in a tight-fitting black skirt, bare legs, and low heels below. Her white blouse made her look like a secretary or librarian.

He'd almost laughed as Nucci made a move on the brunette and it became quickly obvious that he'd been shot down in flames. But the kid had been persistent and had given the woman a business card.

Nucci's back was to him, so he couldn't tell what he said, and Claude had been surprised when she'd leaned forward and given him a light hug, then allowed him to walk along beside her. Playing leapfrog for several blocks, Claude managed to keep them in sight until they stopped in front of a nicely manicured front lawn and talked for a moment. Unbelievably, she followed him up to the porch and into the house.

After sitting there for a couple of hours, Claude had watched Nucci leave again, alone this time, backing out of the one-car garage in a black BMW. Claude got small behind the wheel when the car rolled past. He wasn't worried. It was four o'clock and he knew where the punk was going.

While he'd waited, Claude hadn't concerned himself about the woman Nucci had lured into his house. The punk was the target and she'd have to fend for herself. While he'd waited, he'd devised a better plan for killing the man.

He knew they were going to go for a walk on the beach, but he didn't know where. So, he'd planned to simply follow them and wait until he could confront them on an empty stretch of sand. Then he could just shoot them both.

Or maybe just the guy and take the girl for a little fun ride.

When Nucci turned into the café parking lot, Claude found a spot near it and adjusted his dash camera. Nucci came around the corner and, after greeting the waitress, he'd spoken with her for a bit. She told him she had a customer if he was interested. Then she'd introduced him to two of her friends, a slim blonde dressed in a dark skirt and pale-blue blouse, and a broad-shouldered, hipster-looking guy with a long goatee.

Using his camera, Claude could see the four of them discussing buying drugs, but Nucci had been wary, telling the man that he didn't have anything with him.

Instead, the four made plans to go to a local nightclub and Nucci would bring what they wanted from his car, but only after they'd had a few drinks to get to know them and their operation better.

It seemed that the other couple were also drug dealers.

That twist had wrecked Claude's simple beach murder plan, but he was a patient man. He'd done this kind of thing a few times before. He knew he'd get his chance soon and followed the foursome when they left in Nucci's car. A couple of blocks later, the other couple got out and then followed the BMW in a small blue sports car.

For the last half hour, Claude had been sitting at a table in the corner of a nightclub, watching and waiting.

Of the four, the blond friend of the waitress was the only one facing him. Not directly, but he could see her face best and she occasionally glanced his way.

He could see only the sides of the two men's faces but easily picked up on most of their conversation. Seated against the wall with a hat on, his face was shaded, and he kept his head turned away from their table. There was no way anyone could see his eyes unless they were right in front of him.

He was close enough to decipher most of what they were discussing, and the noisy bar didn't diminish that ability in the least. They seemed to feel comfortable talking openly in low voices, since nobody was close enough to hear over the music and loud voices in the bar.

While he watched the couple, he also watched the men's room, keeping track of who was coming and going there. Sooner or later, the guy would have to piss and that would be the place Claude would kill him. If he went in when it was empty, he wouldn't come out. At least, not without a stretcher and a sheet over his head.

If Claude didn't get the opportunity there, he could wait until the deal was made and the couples split up. He still liked the beach hit; the blond waitress, who he now knew was called Layla, would be a bonus over and above the debt he owed Boudreaux.

Not that the other blonde with them was any slouch. Her name was either Cabby or Gabby, he couldn't be sure. The way both words were pronounced looked almost exactly the same, though Cabby seemed an odd name.

She was a little older than the waitress, but well put together. She glanced over at him again, subtly, but she seemed to study him for a moment. Moving only his eyes, he looked away for a second and when he looked back, she was smiling at the waitress and talking animatedly.

She might have been interested, women looked at him all the time, but she obviously couldn't tell he was watching them.

The man she was with was big, but when he sat, his trouser leg rode up and Claude had noticed he had a fake right leg. Still, that was two more chances that something could go wrong if he tried to take all four.

The two women got up from the table and headed out onto the dance floor, oblivious to his presence.

Nucci asked the man if he had the money and the man nodded. The two of them got up and started toward the bathroom, where they would make the exchange.

ELUSIVE CHARITY

Claude waited a few seconds, his head turned toward the dance floor. After spotting the two blondes swaying to the music, arms raised, he concentrated on the two men. There wasn't anyone else in the bathroom at the moment.

"Fuck it," Claude whispered under his breath as he rose and started to follow them.

Get it done and get out of here, he thought. Chicks like those two were a dime a dozen.

He weaved through the crowd, feeling the weight of the gun and suppressor in his pocket. Following well behind Nucci and the guy with the fake leg, he noticed that the guy moved fairly easily, not limping or anything. The two disappeared into the bathroom as Claude entered the short hallway behind them.

As he stepped through the bathroom door, he pulled his suppressed handgun from his pants pocket and pointed it at the two men.

"Hello, Mr. Nucci," Claude said, taking both men unaware. "Mr. Boudreaux sends his regards."

He aimed the gun at Nucci's chest, but just as he started to squeeze the trigger, the one-legged man pushed Nucci aside, stepping into the line of fire.

The sound the gun made was a barely audible puff, then the empty cartridge was ejected and bounced off a stall door to his right. Both sounds were squelched by the din coming from the bar.

Claude's first shot hit the bigger man. He started to go down and Claude quickly moved the barrel of the short suppressor toward Nucci, now cowering in the corner.

Suddenly, the door flew open and banged off the wall. Before he could turn, Claude took a hard kick between his legs, which doubled him over in pain. His grip on the gun faltered and it skittered across the tile floor toward the man he'd shot.

As his knees buckled and he spun toward the floor, he saw the blonde in the short skirt and frilly blue shirt standing in the doorway, the waitress behind her. The blonde leaned to the side, extending her right foot in a snap kick that caught him in the forehead. Then everything went black.

CHAPTER TWENTY-SIX

"Get his coat off," Charity said, moving quickly to DJ's side, who was struggling to get to a seated position. "Are you okay?"

"Shoulder," he grunted, in obvious pain. "I think it went through."

Charity leaned him forward a little, checking his back. "Yeah, a through and through. It was probably a jacketed round; the exit wound isn't very big."

In the heat of the moment, Charity had dropped the trailer trash accent. She looked over at Nucci, still crouched in the corner, then pointed at the unconscious man on the floor. "Get his jacket off! Now!"

"I'll get it," Layla said, bending to roll the man over.

"Whatta we do with him?" DJ asked, nodding toward the gunman.

"You okay to stand?" Charity asked.

"Yeah," DJ grunted, in obvious pain as he pushed himself up the wall, leaving a streak of blood. He drove his left fist backward at the wall. "Same frickin' place as last time!" he groaned. "Why is it whenever I meet you, I get shot?"

She knew he was just trying to make light of the serious

situation they were in, but the truth in his words still stung. It had happened too many times before, with every man she involved herself with.

"Here," Layla said, extending the man's jacket. "Who was that guy?"

"Put this on," Charity said, holding the coat open for DJ. "Your shirt's got a couple of drops of blood on it."

DJ looked down at his right shoulder. The guayabera had a large red stain down the front. He shrugged his injured arm through the sleeve and Charity helped him get his other arm in, then pulled it up over his broad shoulders. It was actually a little big on him.

She looked down at the man. "I have no idea who he is. But I'm going to wake him up, march him out of here, and find out."

"Just leave him," DJ said, putting the man's gun in the left jacket pocket. "Boudreaux sent him," he added, looking over at Nucci. "He was sent here to kill you for trying to push your way into his territory."

"Wh-who are you?" Nucci asked.

Charity had slipped out of character for a moment, but quickly recovered. "We're just some folks smart enough to not cross Bennett Boudreaux, that's who we are. C'mon, Blunt. Let's get outta here."

"Wait!" Nucci said, getting to his feet. "There might be more of them."

"More of them after *you*, man," DJ said. "Hell with waitin' around. Boudreaux don't know me and I wanna keep it that way. Right now, I'm gonna find a place to get horizontal with a bottle and let Gabby here stitch me up. You're on your own."

The man on the floor moaned and began to stir. Nucci looked down at him, then back up at DJ. "I can pay you."

DJ glanced over at Charity. "Up to you, babe."

She glared at Nucci and pointed to the door. "Go," she said. "We'll take your car." Then she turned to Layla. "Can you drive a stick?"

"Well, sure, but—"

"No buts," DJ said. "You take Gabby's car and go back to the café. That's where you live, right?"

She nodded.

"We'll get it later," Charity said. "You're just an innocent bystander in this and I'm sorry I got you messed up in it."

She looked over at Nucci, then back at Charity. "No, I'm going with you. We can go to my place. Nobody will be around."

The gunman started to push himself up with one hand, trying to roll over, then collapsed back to the floor.

"Out," Charity ordered. "I've got a first aid kit in my car."

Nucci led the way, with Layla behind him, and Charity holding DJ's good arm as if she were leaning on him, but actually, she was helping support him.

They made their way down the hall and started through the crowded bar. A man stumbled and bumped DJ's injured shoulder, causing him to grimace.

"Watch where you're going, asshat!" the man slurred.

Nucci quickly stepped around DJ and Charity. "What did you say to this man, *amico mio*? He works for me!"

The bigger man stepped back, raising both hands, palms out. "Sorry, Mr. Nucci. I don't want no trouble."

"Good," Nucci said, then turned and led the way to the door.

Outside, they moved quickly over to Charity's car, where she opened the trunk. Reaching inside, she pulled out a trauma kit and placed it on the ground.

DJ shrugged out of the coat as Charity closed the trunk, knelt down and opened the small box.

She ripped open a bag of granular QuikClot. "Sit on the car and lean forward."

"C'mon," DJ moaned. "That shit? You don't have clotting bandages?"

He braced himself against the low car, anyway, leaning forward as Charity ordered. She got her fingers in the hole made by the bullet and ripped the fabric apart. Then she poured half the contents of the pouch directly into the open wound.

The burn caused DJ to arch his back in pain. Charity quickly tore open a gauze pad and peeled the backing off, then slapped it in place, and forced DJ back onto the trunk.

"This is my favorite part," she said, hiking her skirt slightly, and straddling his legs. She ripped the front of his shirt open, sending buttons flying across the pavement.

"Somehow, I thought this'd be a little more romantic," DJ said, looking up at her.

Charity leaned over him, her hair brushing his bare chest, then poured the rest of the granules into the entry wound. DJ's eyes rolled back in his head as he gritted his teeth and snarled.

Helping him off her vehicle, Charity pointed toward Nucci's car. "Let's go. Somebody's bound to have found that man by now."

The foursome piled in, with DJ and Charity in the backseat. "Go to Layla's," she said to Nucci. "I need to clean and dress his wounds better."

"Why'd that guy back down like that?" DJ asked, leaning back against the seat, and easing his good shoulder against Charity.

As Nucci drove, he seemed to regain the attitude he'd had before cowering in the corner of the bathroom. "People in this town respect *La Famiglia*."

The Mafia? Charity asked herself. What the hell had they gotten themselves into? Then, remembering how active the drug dealer was on social media, she immediately doubted the veracity of his claim. Organized crime didn't put itself out there so openly.

Nucci drove back to the café at a safe, though often excessive speed, like he was trying to prove something with his car. Darkness had fallen and when they arrived, the place was dark, except for a light at the top of the outside stairs.

"Up this way," Layla said, hurrying toward the steps as she fumbled with her keys.

Nucci made a move back toward his car. "I think I will call it a—"

"Oh, no you don't, *amico mio*," DJ grunted. "I think there's probably safety in numbers. You stay with us."

"I think I can—"

"We still have a deal to make," Charity said. "And then there's that whole hiring business you mentioned to get you out of there."

"Very well," he said, following after the waitress. "But I would have had no problem leaving there without you."

"Except you didn't," Charity said, picking up the first aid kit and helping DJ toward the steps.

Above, Layla opened the door and stepped inside, turning on an interior light. Then she came back out and held the door open for them.

"Close the blinds," Charity ordered, as she moved DJ to the small kitchenette and seated him in a chair.

After completely removing DJ's shirt, she had him lean forward in the chair, so she could get to his exit wound. Then she carefully peeled the bandage off, noting that the hole was slightly larger than she'd first thought. A scar next to it spoke volumes. It was quite a bit larger.

The bleeding had stopped, as she'd known it would, so she used a swab to clean the area around the exit wound, leaving only the purplish glob of coagulated blood and QuikClot in the middle. Then she wiped his skin all around the wound with a dry cloth and applied a fresh bandage.

"Okay, sit back," she ordered. "Let me do your front."

Though he was grimacing in pain, he still managed a semi-lewd grin. "Oh, baby!"

"Shut up," she said, pushing him back in the chair. "You're lucky. It doesn't look like the bullet hit the bone or anything vital."

DJ twisted his neck, trying to see. "Yeah, well, a couple of inches to the left and he'd have hit my head."

"Like I said," Charity responded, as she quickly went to work on the entry wound, "he didn't hit a bone or anything vital."

She cleaned the wound carefully and soon had a fresh bandage in place on his upper chest.

"It wasn't *exactly* the same place," she said. "But it'll look like a single scar. Maybe you could get an infinity tattoo around them."

"Real funny," DJ said, picking up his guayabera from the floor and shaking it at her. "You ruined my shirt."

"No, the hitman ruined your shirt, Blunt," Charity replied. "Want me to send Boudreaux the bill?"

"I have a couple of shirts that might fit," Layla offered.

"That'd be real sweet," DJ said, mustering a smile.

She disappeared into the bedroom.

"You two seem to be pretty...capable," Nucci said, a tinge of wariness in his voice.

"Not our first rodeo," DJ said. "Y'all down here ain't got nothin' on them boys back up in the hills."

"Where exactly did you say you were from?" Nucci asked, as

Layla came back into the room.

"Here, try this," she said, opening a black, long-sleeved shirt with snaps instead of buttons.

"I didn't," DJ said, allowing Layla to pull the right sleeve of the shirt up his arm. "But if you're asking, we met at a truck stop, Johnson City, Tennessee."

Layla got DJ's good arm through the sleeve and helped get it up over the bandages. He winced slightly.

"Were you gassing up your Firebird?" Layla asked, sardonically.

DJ grinned at her, appreciating that she'd caught the Travis Tritt reference. "Just a *Modern Day Bonny and Clyde*," he said, turning toward her. "I'm afraid you'll have to do the honors. I seem to be without the use of my right arm."

"I'll take care of that," Charity said, stepping in front of her. "If you have some scissors, maybe you could cut Blunt's old shirt up into a couple of long strips to make a sling."

She scurried off and DJ smiled as Charity fastened each snap, starting at the top. "Ya know, a guy could get used to all this pamperin' real easy."

"I suppose I should thank you," Nucci said. "Like the drunk in the bar, most people around here know who I am. So, how long have the two of you worked together?"

Layla returned with a pair of scissors and got to work rending DJ's shirt into strips. He looked down at the Western style shirt he had on, with pearl snaps down the front and on the pocket flaps, then glared at Charity.

"Twelve years," Charity replied, smiling at him. "As of last month."

"And I don't know how many of my shirts ended up like that in those twelve years," DJ said. "She wasn't kiddin' when she said she liked to rip my shirt off."

Charity turned back to the table, picking up the mess, a bit of color in her cheeks. "You oughta wear them snap kind more."

Layla moved behind DJ and slung his good arm, tying it off behind his neck at a comfortable length. "This'll give us the right length without hurting too much."

Lifting his prosthetic leg, DJ kicked a chair with what would have been his shin. The impact made a muffled metallic ring and the chair bounced across the floor.

"Don't you worry none about ol' Blunt," he said, smiling at the girl. Then he glared at Charity. "I got a real high tolerance for pain."

CHAPTER TWENTY-SEVEN

A dark-blue-and-gray Ford pickup turned off Main Street, headed north on Baylen. Two men were in the truck, the passenger staring vacantly through the side window as they rolled past the exit of a small drive-thru café.

"This'll be the third time we've gone to his house," Lucas said from behind the wheel.

He glanced over at his friend. Leo was a mess when he was drunk; now he was just tired and mean.

"He's gotta show up sooner or later," Leo replied, still staring out the window. "We'll just keep drivin' back and forth between his house and his strip club till we find him."

"That could be hours," Lucas said, shifting to second gear. "Or even days, maybe. Are you sure he owns that club?"

"He does," Leo replied.

Two blocks later, Lucas turned left, then took the first right, then left again. Leo sat up and pointed. "Was that light on before?"

Lucas slowed.

"Pull over," Leo said. "I don't think it was."

"There ain't no car in the carport, man."

"Maybe he rode home with someone or walked," Leo insisted. "It's less than a mile. Pull over!"

Lucas's brakes squealed a little as he slowed and pulled to the curb a couple of houses past the drug dealer's place. "It was barely dark last time," he said. "The light might've been on and we didn't notice it."

"I wanna check it out."

"You're nuts, man. What if a cop comes by?"

Leo turned his head and glared at Lucas. "She was my sister, bruh!"

"Okay," Lucas said, shutting off the engine. "We'll both go. One person waitin' just looks suspicious."

The street was mostly residential, though the two houses on the corner had been converted to businesses, and it looked like a couple of the properties on this block were running businesses out of the homes.

Though it was barely ten o'clock, most of the houses were dark. A single streetlight a few driveways farther down lit the middle part of the block.

Lucas and Leo got out of the truck, the hinges squeaking as the doors opened and closed, then walked back toward Antoine Nucci's house.

Finding out who the guy was hadn't been all that hard. Lucas and Leo called around to everyone they knew, and the same first name Karin had told Lucas popped up twice. Then one of Leo's buddies put a last name to the guy. The rest was easy—he was all over Instagram and Facebook.

The porch was dark and there were no lights visible through the front windows. The one they'd seen was coming from a small window at ground level on the side.

"A basement?" Leo asked rhetorically.

"Not many of those in Florida," Lucas said. "He probably just forgot to turn the light off."

"Let's check it out."

Leo started to move up the driveway, but Lucas grabbed his shoulder. "This guy's a drug dealer, man. Drives a fancy black BMW, throws money around, and probably has guns."

"Then keep the noise down," Leo said, jerking away.

Lucas went after him, muttering, "This is nuts, dude."

Once beside the house, the two were quickly enveloped in shadows and Lucas felt a little safer. They crept slowly toward the source of the light—a window recessed in a brick-lined hole with gravel at the bottom.

Leo got down on his hands and knees for a better look. The top of the window was about ground level, and looking over his shoulder, all Lucas could see was a bare concrete floor. The light from the window illuminated Leo's face and Lucas saw his mouth fall open.

"What is it?" Lucas whispered.

His friend scooted over slightly, angling for a better view. "See for yourself, bruh."

When Lucas got low enough to peer into the basement room, the first thing his eyes fell on was an unmade bed and someone lying in it, but all he could make out were two bare legs.

"It's a woman," Leo whispered, having a better angle. "She's freakin' tied to the bed, man."

Seeing the ropes around the woman's ankles sent a shiver up Lucas's spine. "Let's get the hell out of here, man."

The two walked quickly back to the street, then down the sidewalk toward Lucas's truck, both of them casting furtive glances over their shoulders.

"What do you think's going on?" Leo asked. "Just a kinky couple and he forgot to untie her?"

Lucas looked doubtfully at him. "Yeah, I bet that happens all the time."

Suddenly, Leo froze in his tracks. "Wait a minute."

"Wait, hell!" Lucas whisper-shouted. "We need to get out of here, find a pay phone, and report this to the cops."

"Did you say he drove a black BMW?"

"Yeah. So?"

Leo looked back the way they'd come. "There was one behind that coffee shop on the corner."

"What coffee shop, man?" Lucas asked, desperation raising the pitch in his voice to a whine.

"On the main drag. Where we turned into the neighborhood here."

"I didn't see any—"

"You weren't looking," Leo said, hurrying toward the truck's passenger side.

Lucas raced after him and climbed in the driver's seat. At Leo's insistence, he drove around the block and went back the way they'd come in.

"Slow down," Leo said, pointing ahead and to the left. "The entrance is just before the corner on that side."

As they approached, Lucas saw *One Way* and *Do Not Enter* signs. He looked in his mirror—there wasn't anyone behind them.

"That's the exit," he said, his brakes squeaking as he stopped fifty feet before the intersection.

Just as Leo had said, he spotted the same car he'd seen on the night Karin died. It was parked close to the building and facing the wrong way for a one-way alley.

"Is that his car?" Leo asked.

"Could be," Lucas replied. "Looks like the same model, at least."

"It's a drive-thru coffee shop," Leo said. "Everything's closed, though. Go ahead and pull in the wrong way and we'll check it out."

"What if a cop—"

"I came here to kill this fucker," Leo snarled. "And you're worried about a traffic ticket?"

CHAPTER TWENTY-EIGHT

The squeak of brakes from the side street caught Charity's attention. It wasn't so much the sound—they'd heard a number of vehicles go by on both streets—it was more where this one had stopped that was different.

DJ noticed it too, his head snapping toward the window.

Someone had stopped well short of the intersection.

DJ quickly pulled his left arm from the sling and grabbed the suppressed Glock from the pocket of the jacket draped over a chair beside him.

Charity raised her skirt and pulled the DB9 from its holster, holding it in both hands in the low ready position. She glanced over at DJ, who started to move toward the window, then she moved quickly to the door.

She knew that normally, DJ would probably have preferred his own Kimber in his hand. But with his right arm dangling pretty much useless, the smaller caliber 9mm, with the added barrel length of the suppressor would be far easier for him to manage off-handed than the cannon she knew was under his shirt.

"Kill the lights," DJ hissed.

Charity smacked the light switch by the door, then pressed her back to the wall next to it, looking through the small half-circle window in the upper part of the door. "You two get down on the floor," she said to Nucci and Layla.

Across the room, DJ assumed a similar stance by the window overlooking the side street. He leaned close and used the suppressor to raise one of the slats in the blind.

"Dark-colored Ford pickup pulling in the exit," DJ said. "Early-to mid-1980's model."

"A 1985 F150, maybe?" she asked.

He glanced over at her, lines of moonlight crossing his face from the waxing crescent moon shining through the slats. "That's an awfully specific question, babe. You expecting somebody?"

"Maybe," she replied, cracking the door open slightly.

She could just see Nucci's car near the bottom of the steps as headlights washed over the expensive sedan, then a pickup angled in front of it, the brakes squeaking when it stopped. When the doors opened, the truck's inside light came on and Charity instantly recognized the driver.

"Lucas Rivera," she said, though not recognizing the other man he was with.

"The kid you told me about from Apalach?" DJ asked. "What's he doin' here?"

"My guess is," she began, looking over at the drug dealer squatting on the floor, "he and the guy with him came here to kill Mr. Nucci. You two stay put," she ordered. "And maybe you need to give Blunt a number to start the protection deal negotiations." She opened the door fully and looked down. "Coz, I don't see any *La Famiglia* down there."

"Wait," DJ blurted. "What are you gonna—"

"I know them," Charity said, flipping the outside light back on. "And I know how to get rid of them."

ELUSIVE CHARITY

Charity put her hands behind her back, holding the DB9 between them, and started walking slowly down the steps, allowing her hips to sway more than normal to make sure she had their attention.

The two were examining Nucci's car, but they'd both looked up quickly as she'd turned the light on, and they were now staring at her coming down the steps.

"Hi, Lucas," Charity said, reaching the bottom of the steps and stopping ten feet away from the two young men.

The second one seemed a few years older, maybe mid-twenties. He was also taller and a bit heavier. She saw no evidence of a weapon and didn't feel either was much of a threat.

She moved her weight slowly from one foot to the other. "I hope your friend Kenny recovered okay. Who did you bring with you tonight?"

"What're you do—?" Rivera started to ask before his friend cut him off.

"Who the fuck are *you*, lady?" the other guy snapped, standing slightly behind Rivera.

She took two slow, seductive steps toward the two men. So far, they hadn't brandished a weapon, but Charity doubted they'd come looking for Nucci empty-handed. What other reason would they have for being there?

"Lucas," she said softly, "please explain to your friend that I don't like loud-mouthed little boys."

Lucas raised a hand to his side, palm back, blocking the other man, should he decide to move. "Be quiet, Leo. This's the lady PI, I told you about—the one who knocked Kenny out."

He moved to Rivera's right, distancing himself. "Yeah, well we're both ready now," he said. "You think you can take on two men?"

Charity glanced over and cocked a hip. "Both of you at once? That could be fun."

His slow, flanking movement halted for a second as his eyes moved down Charity's body. "The question is, what are you doing here with the guy who killed my sister?"

Charity took another step toward Lucas, allowing the one he'd called Leo, and who it seemed was the brother of the dead girl, Karin, to flank her a little, just out of arm's reach.

It was an intentional move, designed to lure the bigger man closer, while her attention was fully on Rivera.

Leo feigned a lunge toward her, probably just to see what she'd do, and though he was still out of arm's reach, the move had put him within range of her feet.

Charity had long, athletic legs—a thirty-six inseam—and when she spun and executed a snap kick, she caught Leo just below the ear. She finished the spin and brought her gun up, pointed at Lucas's chest.

She didn't need to look behind her to be sure that Leo had gone down—the thunk of meat on pavement told her all she needed to know.

"This is getting old, Lucas," she said, stepping close enough to put the barrel under his chin. "You keep hanging around rude men, it might change you."

He froze, craning his chin upward and extending both hands to his sides, fingers spread wide, as if she'd touched him with a cattle prod.

"Remember what I told you about me asking questions I already know the answer to?"

He nodded.

"Good. Did Antoine Nucci sell you the drugs that Karin Bishop overdosed on?"

He nodded again, saucer-eyed in fear.

"You get a gold star," she said. "I already knew that. That's why *I'm* here. Now, why are *you* here?"

He gulped. "Leo wanted to find Antoine Nucci."

Charity smiled, but there was nothing in her eyes that revealed any sort of mirth. "Very good, Lucas. Is that insolent young man really Karin's brother?"

Once more, Rivera's head bobbed. "Leo Bishop," he croaked.

"When he wakes up, you'll apologize for me?"

"You're...letting us go?"

"If you promise to go back to Apalach," Charity replied, hearing an uneven clomping coming down the steps behind her. "You're way out of your league here."

"You're never gonna see me again," he promised.

"Everything okay, here?" DJ asked, coming up beside her.

"Check that guy," Charity said, cocking her head to the left.

"You guys must be gluttons for punishment, kid," DJ said to Rivera, as he turned toward Bishop. "You really don't wanna see this lady when she's angry."

N-no...no, I don't," Lucas stammered.

Charity slowly lowered her weapon, holding it loosely at her side, but ready. "Are you armed?"

"There's a rifle in my truck," he replied.

"Is it yours?"

"My dad's," he replied.

"Back up," Charity ordered, putting her left hand on Lucas's chest, and marching him backward. She pointed at the rear tire. "Over there."

Lucas complied, and with him standing five feet away, Charity

209

opened the driver's side door, glancing quickly inside. She saw nothing out of the ordinary.

"Where?" she asked, looking back at Lucas.

"Behind the seat," he replied sullenly. "The catch is at the bottom. Just pull it up."

Charity looked and saw the release, then pulled up on it, flipping the seat forward. Behind it was mounted a double gun rack for shotguns or hunting rifles. It held a single bolt-action rifle—an antique .30-30 carbine.

"Nothing on that guy," DJ said, joining her beside the truck.

"Watch him," Charity said, as she leaned in and retrieved the rifle.

DJ pointed the suppressed Glock at the younger man. "You two working alone?" he asked in a friendly voice. His next words came out like ice. "Or were you helping the guy I took this gun from *after* he shot me with it?"

Charity stood and removed the magazine from the rifle, placing it on the seat, then looked over at Rivera. She racked the bolt expertly, but no cartridge came out.

"I'd answer him honestly, Lucas," she said, putting the rifle back in the rack. "You only get one chance at it."

"I don't know anything about anyone else," he said. "Honest. Me and Leo just came up here to find Nucci. Leo wanted to kick his ass for selling us some high-grade stuff without telling us how strong it was."

"You believe him?" DJ asked.

"Yeah, I believe him," Charity replied, gently removing the cartridges from the magazine, and tossing it onto the floorboard before looking at Rivera. "And I also believe he's stupid enough to do just what his friend asked him to do."

210

"Whatta ya wanna do with them?" DJ asked, as Bishop moaned and began to stir.

"Let them go," Charity replied, turning a blistering gaze toward Rivera, and pointing at Bishop. "Get him in your truck, drive back home to Apalach, and forget about revenge. It's elusive at best and you two don't have the stomach for it."

Rivera scooted past DJ and went over to Leo, helping him to his feet. Bishop was still groggy and staggered like a drunk as Lucas helped him to the passenger seat.

When he came back around the hood, he stopped beside the open door, facing Charity. "There's something you oughta know," he said.

"What's that?" Charity asked.

Rivera looked up at the apartment and lowered his voice. "Is Nucci up there?"

Charity glanced at DJ then back at Rivera. "He is."

"He has a woman tied up in the basement of his house."

CHAPTER TWENTY-NINE

As the truck slowly backed out into the street, DJ turned to Charity and said, "This changes things considerably."

"It sure does," she replied, looking up at the apartment. "Do you think you can hoof it over to his house while I keep him busy here?"

He grinned. "I didn't bring my hoofin' leg, either. But I think I can manage. The shoulder hurts like hell, but thanks to you, I didn't lose much blood, unlike the last time. I'm good to go."

"Be careful," she said. "And call me when you know something."

"Aw, Charity, you *do* care," he said.

"Just don't get caught by the cops while prowling around his house," she admonished, then smiled. "If you do, I'll personally kick your ass."

"Still looking forward to that," he said with a mischievous grin. "But after seeing how you took that guy out, I will say the thought makes me a little nervous. So, I won't bother asking if you'll be okay."

"If she's dead, wipe everything down that you touch, and we can find a pay phone to call it in. If she's hurt, we'll have to get her help and maybe not involve the police directly. I can call someone with the Franklin County Sheriff's Office, and they can get the information to local law enforcement."

She helped him get his arm into the sling, then stashed the suppressed Glock there as well.

"Be back in a few minutes," he said, then turned and walked down the street into a semi-residential neighborhood.

Charity climbed back up the stairs and into the apartment, where she turned the lights on again and closed and locked the door.

"What happened?" Nucci asked. "Who were they?"

"Sit down," Charity said, and pulled a chair over to the couch. "Both of you."

They sat on the couch and Charity looked from one to the other, trying to decide the girl's involvement and what to do with Nucci. If what Rivera said was true, and DJ found a woman tied up in his basement, she knew what she'd *like* to do with him.

"They're gone and won't come back," she began. "But let's back up to the beginning. How long have the two of you been seeing each other?"

"We hardly know one another," Layla said with a sigh. "Tonight was my first date since a bad breakup in February." She rubbed her knees, then dropped her hands into her lap. "Heck of a new beginning, huh?"

Charity turned to face her. "You thought it would be a clever idea to set up a drug deal for the guy you were going out with?"

She looked over at Nucci, then back at Charity. "I knew he sold some here and there," she admitted. "I guess...I don't know...I thought he might appreciate a referral."

Charity turned to face the man. "Do you even know what you're selling?"

He became indignant. "I don't have to answer to you," he said and started to rise.

But Charity was on her feet before him and grabbed his shirt front. She smacked him sharply across the face and forced him backward. With the couch there, his only option was to fall back onto it.

Layla gasped and leaned away.

"Yeah, you do," Charity said quietly, straightening his shirt. "And before you go mouthing about mafia connections, don't waste your breath. You're no more *La Famiglia* than I am.

The shocked look on his face told her that he was unaccustomed to being bullied. Which meant he had some clout, even if it was just in his own mind. But she was sure he wasn't a true mafioso. Perhaps he'd used the lie so much he actually believed it himself.

"I'll ask again," she said in a quiet tone, sitting back down on the kitchen chair. "Do you know what you're selling to those kids?"

"What are you? A cop?"

"No, I'm not a cop," she replied, lifting her skirt slightly to pull the DB9 from its holster. "But I'm more than happy to finish the job those two men and Boudreaux's man came here to do."

Charity held the gun loosely in her hand, resting it on her lap.

Nucci stared at it for a moment before locking eyes with her. "I provide a product," he replied in a sullen tone. "Sometimes it's weed, sometimes it's pills."

"Let's talk about those pills," she said. "A little over a week ago, you sold a quantity of oxy to a girl named Karin Bishop over in Carrabelle. Remember her?"

"She was a regular for a while," he said. "But moved away. She contacted me two weeks ago and said she was back."

"So, you met her and her friends at an abandoned farm and sold them some oxy. Is that about right?"

"What's in this for you?"

"Closure," she replied. "The pills you sold her had the letters IR on the back. Do you know what that means?"

"Indiana Railroad?" he asked, flippantly. "Whaddo I give a shit?"

Charity hung her head and shook it slowly before looking back at the man. "Karin Bishop took two ten-milligram *immediate release* tablets you sold her, thinking they were the usual five-milligram slow dissolving, and she was dead in a matter of minutes."

Layla's face drained of color. "She overdosed?"

Charity nodded, without taking her eyes off Nucci. "One of those tablets would knock a big man like Blunt out cold in less than a minute. Two would be fatal within an hour."

"How'm I supposed to know?" Nucci said. "I'm not a pharmacist. All I do is provide the product. I don't tell people how many to take."

Charity glared at the man with intense loathing. "Monday afternoon, a fifteen-year-old boy on vacation with his family over on St. George Island overdosed on the same tablets."

Layla leaned back, moving away from Nucci. "You're a monster!" she shouted, then rose to her feet. "What'd I ever see in you?"

He ignored her. "You're not a dealer from Tennessee, are you?" he asked.

"No," Charity replied. "I'm from California. And I'm not another drug dealer, either."

"So, what are you?"

"I'm a private investigator," she replied. "Hired by the dead boy's father to find out why he died. Now I'll have to tell him his boy died because some turd-fondler couldn't be bothered to warn his customers what the dosage was."

"Get out!" Layla shouted. "Get out of my house and never come

216

back to my café."

"Sit back down," Charity said. "Nobody's going anywhere until I hear from my partner. I still haven't decided what your involvement is in all this."

She started to protest, but Charity cut her off with a glance from her cold blue eyes. "Drug dealing isn't Antoine's only crime."

CHAPTER THIRTY

DJ pocketed his phone after walking around the last corner; the GPS app told him his destination was one hundred feet ahead. A law office stood on the corner with a consignment store across from it. The rest of the block appeared to be just homes. But most were dark and several had work trucks and vans with logos on the doors.

His shoulder throbbed but keeping it immobile and suspended in the sling helped. The last time he'd been shot, he'd foolishly—and drunkenly—walked several miles to Dep's house, but Dep wasn't there, and the place had been ransacked. Jerry'd found him on the back porch and took him back to his boat, *Wayward*, where his wife had patched up his wounds, but he'd lost a lot of blood.

When Charity had gone down to confront the two men, he'd stood in the apartment's doorway, watching. She'd stepped too close to the Rivera kid and allowed the other guy to get around her. DJ had a clean shot at him and when he'd lunged at her, he'd almost fired. But in the fraction of a second it took him to take the slack out of the trigger, the other guy was face down on the ground and she had her gun under Rivera's chin. He'd never seen anyone move with such lightning quickness.

"What the hell did I go and get into this time?" he muttered to himself as a car drove past.

He waved nonchalantly.

What was it about Charity Styles that pulled so hard at him? She was perfectly capable; she'd demonstrated that with great ease. And he'd heard the stories about a couple of her assignments. But they'd been unsubstantiated rumors up to now. To say she was a dangerous woman would be a huge understatement. Word got around. Some called her a ticking time bomb because of what'd happened to her in Afghanistan.

He didn't see that. Sure, she might go off one day and take a dozen people with her, but it wasn't a matter of *time*. It was more like the stupid IED that had taken his leg. He'd stepped on a trigger. If and when Charity Styles lost it and went off, it would be because someone tripped *her* trigger.

"And there's the fact that she's smokin' hot," he said under his breath, checking the address on the house he was walking past.

I wonder how many guys got into situations way over their head because of a hot girl? DJ thought, as he spotted the address on the mailbox of the house the kid from Apalach had given them.

It was a low-roofed, single-story home of concrete blocks and stucco, typical for homes built in the 1950s or 60s along much of Florida's coastline—stout little houses that could withstand a hurricane.

The fact that it had a basement set it apart from about ninety-eight percent of all the other houses in the state within ten miles of the coast. Groundwater was usually less than ten feet down and basements were impractical.

DJ saw the light from the side of the house, as Rivera had described. He checked the street both ways, then moved quickly up the driveway and into the shadow of a cluster of small palms bordering the next property.

The yard was surrounded by tropical foliage, well-maintained, and thick enough to cast deep shadows from the streetlight a few houses down.

He moved over to the wall and approached the lighted basement window, recessed into a French drain. Kneeling, he could see inside and sure enough, he saw a woman's legs tied to a bed, unmoving.

Getting to his feet, DJ pulled the Glock from its hiding place with his left hand, then turned and walked toward the back of the house. There he found a six-foot wooden privacy fence with a gate. He softly rattled the handle, hoping he wouldn't encounter a barking dog.

Hearing nothing, he checked the latch. It was unlocked.

DJ quietly opened the gate and stepped into the backyard. It was larger than he would have thought—narrow, but very deep—and surrounded on all sides by a six-foot fence and dense shrubbery. There was even a swimming pool. He moved toward a covered back porch and found a sliding glass door.

"This is too easy," he said under his breath, assessing the door.

It was locked, but that kind of door was a burglar's dream. He put the toe of his left foot lightly against the glass, then jerked up on the handle, while pressing harder with his foot to keep the door from dropping back down onto its rollers. The door lifted off the latch, and he simply slid it open.

No alarm sounded and he wasn't met by a growling Doberman, but that didn't mean there wasn't a monitored silent alarm. If there was, Charity was with Nucci and the security company would call him. It would be up to her to force him to tell them to turn it off and ignore it.

The room he'd entered was a dining room with a connected kitchen. Together, they flowed into a large living room with two doors on each side. DJ went left, where both doors stood open. The first one was a small half-bath—just a commode and a sink—and the other door opened to a bedroom with its own full bathroom.

He crossed the living room and opened one of the other doors to find a hallway. Leading with the Glock, he checked the two open rooms on the left, two more bedrooms.

Opening two more doors on the right side of the hall revealed a second bathroom and a linen closet.

DJ retraced his steps and opened the last door off the living room. Darkened stairs led down to the basement, where light spilled onto the landing at the bottom from beneath a door.

Slowly descending the steps in the darkness, taking each step down with his good leg to feel the edges of the steps, he soon reached the bottom. The door was locked, but it wasn't any kind of security door or anything and it was hinged so it opened into the room.

Putting the pistol back into his sling, DJ got his wallet out and fumbled with it one-handed until he extracted a thin piece of flexible metal the size of a credit card.

It only took a moment, slipping the metal card behind the jamb with his right hand and pushing and pulling the doorknob with his left before the door fell open.

Dropping his jimmying tool, DJ pulled the Glock back out and stepped into the room. He wasn't prepared for what he found.

The room was lit by two fluorescent fixtures hanging from a bare wood-beam ceiling. One wall held a collection of accoutrements you'd expect to find in a pervert's dungeon. Whips, riding crops, handcuffs, coils of rope, and some things he had no idea about hung from nails.

There was a table below the single window and a bed on either side of it. One was empty, and on the other lay a dark-haired woman, who was tied hand and foot to the four posts.

She appeared to be sleeping and her clothes were disheveled— her blouse partially open and her skirt pushed up.

DJ stuck the gun back in his sling, moved quickly to the side of the bed, and checked her wrist for a pulse. It was strong and steady, but his touch didn't wake her.

Feeling somewhat insecure, he reached over and pulled the woman's skirt back down into place then pulled her blouse together. Neither was a smart thing to do from a forensic standpoint. Dep had at least taught him that. But DJ had crossed that bridge when he broke into the house.

He nudged the woman's shoulder. "Miss?"

She didn't stir, so he cupped her chin and patted her cheek very lightly. "Miss? Wake up."

Her eyes opened partially, unfocused, and she moaned.

Some kind of drug or something, DJ thought, then moved over to the table beside the bed. The window over it had a heavy drape and he pulled it closed. The last thing he wanted was anyone else peeking in and seeing him.

Pulling open the middle drawer of the writing desk, he found a bunch of old bills and correspondence, along with a pill bottle. He picked the plastic bottle up and opened it, shaking a few tablets out into his hand.

Then he read the label: *Oxycontin, 20mg, extended release. To be taken orally once a day before bed.* The prescription was for someone named Oscar King, Jr.

DJ knew a little bit about oxycodone from personal experience, after losing his foot. He'd been on it for weeks in the hospital in Germany.

He also knew that Oxycontin was the brand name for one type of oxycodone and that it only came in extended release.

He examined the five pills in his hand. Two had a 20 on one side and two had a 10. The last one said 10 IR.

Dumping the rest on the table, he found that most were 20-milligram extended-release Oxycontin tablets, but there were quite a few 10-milligram doses mixed in, and two were 10-milligram immediate release.

"Dumbass probably didn't even know they came in different dosages," he said aloud, shaking his head. Putting pills of different dosages and types of release in the same container was a recipe for disaster.

He looked over at the girl, realizing that she might have ended up a victim of a deadly game of dosage roulette.

DJ pulled a lock-blade knife from his pocket, then slipped it between the brunette's right leg and the rope, parting it easily. He repeated the process three more times, and she still hadn't roused.

He patted her on the cheek a bit harder.

Miss?" he said more forcefully, shaking her shoulder.

Suddenly her eyes came fully open and she drew her arms and legs in, pushing herself toward the corner away from him.

"It's okay, you're all right," DJ said, soothingly. "I'm here to help you. Antoine Nucci isn't here."

"Wh...who are you?" she asked, sounding as if her tongue was dry and swollen.

"My name's Bobbie," he replied, slowly going down to one knee, his good one, to be at eye level with the frightened woman. "I work with a private investigator and I'm going to get you home. Would you like that?"

"Wh...where's that other guy?"

"My partner has him," DJ said. "Do you remember how you got here?"

Her head fell into her hands, and she sobbed.

"Hang in there," DJ said, soothingly. "I promise you're safe now. Can you get up?"

She looked up at him, then down at her wrists. "I was tied up. He...he drugged me and tied me to the bed...then he—"

"Shh," DJ hushed, not wanting to hear any details. "It's all over now. Can you tell me your name? Where you live? How you got here?"

She suddenly lunged toward him, wrapping her arms tightly around his neck. DJ nearly lost his balance but managed to push himself erect, pulling her up to a standing position with him as she cried on his shoulder.

"It's okay, it's okay," he kept saying, holding her and stroking the back of her head with his one good hand, while trying to ignore the crushing pain she was causing.

"Um, miss," he finally said. "You're hurtin' my shoulder."

She stepped back suddenly, her eyes red and makeup-stained tears rolling down both cheeks. Then she noticed his arm in the sling.

"It's okay," he said again. "I hurt it earlier this evening, so it's still a bit tender."

"My name's Joanne," she said between sobs, wiping her face with her hands. "Joanne Mitchell. I was walking...going back to my office when this...this guy came up and said he was a psychologist specializing in divorce trauma."

Pulling his phone from his pocket, DJ asked, "Can I take your picture to send to my partner? She's very worried about you."

"She?"

"My partner's a woman," he replied, raising his phone with a questioning look. "She used to be a cop in Miami."

Joanne nodded as she looked around, and DJ took a quick snapshot to send to Charity to show the woman was okay. Then he had an idea.

"Can you walk?" he asked. "I sure hope so, 'cause I'll be honest." He hiked up his pant leg, showing her the prosthetic, "I don't think I can carry you up those stairs with just one leg and one arm."

CHAPTER THIRTY-ONE

From her small purse, sitting on the kitchen table, Charity heard her phone trilling. She rose and moved backward to it, keeping an eye on Nucci. Using her left hand, she opened it and pulled her phone out before returning to the living room.

"What the hell you mean that's not my only crime?" Nucci demanded, nervous indignation in his voice. "You can't go throwing vague accusations around like that, not even if you are a PI."

Charity opened the text from DJ and read it.

She's alive.

The phone trilled again and a photo appeared. It was a picture of a young, dark-haired woman in a white blouse and black pencil skirt. She was standing beside a bed, where ropes were tied to the four posts.

A moment later, two more pictures appeared. The first showed the same woman, now standing in a well-lit living room next to an open front door. The last picture was of her standing outside on a porch, where a light from her side cast shadows across her face, but she was still easily recognizable. Between her and the light, the address Lucas Rivera had given them was visible.

Smart idea, Charity thought. If it goes to court, photos of the victim inside Nucci's house would be damning evidence.

In the following text message, DJ wrote, *Her name is Joanne Mitchell and her car is at her office a few blocks from here. We're going there.*

"You ask for proof?" Charity said, tapping the photo from the living room to enlarge it. She turned the phone around and thrust it in Nucci's face. "I think Joanne Mitchell might have something to say."

His face went white and he started to stammer.

"Joanne?" Layla said, shocked. "What's she got to do with this?"

"Your *date* abducted her," Charity said, rage beginning to build in the pit of her stomach. "He held her in the basement of his house where he raped her."

"That's a lie!" Nucci shouted.

Charity's gun came up, pointed right at his head. "You have the right to shut the hell up! If you give up that right, I have no compunction about shooting you dead."

Layla wretched, covering her mouth with her hand. It was the reaction Charity had hoped for from her.

"You can go to the bathroom if you feel you're going to be sick."

"No, I'm okay," Layla said, composing herself. "She was at my café today, meeting her divorce lawyer, and Antoine asked about her."

"Is that right?" Charity asked, slowly turning to face the man, her eyes like cold, blue lasers. "Premeditation? The evidence just keeps piling up."

"Your partner broke into my house," he said. "That's illegal search and seizure. Nothing he found there will be admissible in court."

"If it were up to me," Charity hissed, "This would never go to court."

"I have rights!" Nucci shouted belligerently.

"Yeah, you do!" Charity screamed, coming to her feet in an instant. "I said you have the right to shut your piehole. If you give up that right one more time, unless I ask you a question, I'll put a bullet in your brain, so help me."

In truth, the last thing Charity wanted or needed was to have the authorities looking for a fake PI who killed a drug dealer and lived on a sailboat. She'd only intended to dig around a little and give Mr. Conti the name of the man who'd sold his friend's son the drugs.

Layla raised a hand like an obedient schoolgirl. "Do I have to sit next to him?"

"No," Charity replied, having decided that she wasn't involved in the drug-selling beyond trying to impress a guy on the first date. "In fact, do you have any rope?"

"Not rope," she replied. "But I just replaced the blinds in my bedroom and the old one has pull cords."

"That'll do," Charity said. "Grab those scissors and go cut me off as much of it as you can. I need it to tie his hands until Blunt gets back and then we can figure out what to do with him."

Layla got up from the couch and went to the kitchen. She paused as she picked up the scissors, then slowly turned around. "If you want my vote, I think you should take him out in the bay and drown him."

Charity grinned as the younger woman disappeared into the bedroom. Then she looked over at Nucci.

"Funny," she commented. "That was exactly where Bennett Boudreaux said you'd end up."

"That's the second time you've brought up that name," Nucci said, lowering his gaze to the floor. "And that guy at the club mentioned him. Who is he?"

"You don't know him?"

"Should I?"

"If I had to guess," Charity began, as Layla returned, "I'd say he's the closest thing this part of Florida has to a mafia don. You were cutting into his territory. I only met him yesterday—scary guy—but he predicted you'd be floating in the bay before I could find you."

"Lucky me," he said. "You got here first."

"Stand up slowly," Charity ordered, raising her weapon, and levelling it at the man's chest. "If you make any sudden move, I'll kill you."

"You ever use that thing?" Nucci asked, as he slowly rose from the couch.

"The last man who asked me that question is dead," she replied, not showing any emotion as she rose right along with him. "Turn around, kneel on the couch, with your ankles crossed. Put your chest against the back of it and your hands behind you."

He did as she ordered and Charity placed her gun on her chair, hoping he would try something stupid.

He did.

As Charity approached him with nylon cords in her left hand, he twisted and swung a wild backhand toward her face. She was ready for the attack, even hoping for it, and easily blocked his swing. She then delivered a focus punch to the side of his head.

Nucci's body went limp, and Layla screamed.

"It's okay," she told the younger woman. "I wanted him to try. It'll make tying him up a lot easier. Would you get me a glass of water, please?"

"I have bottled water."

"It's not for me," Charity said, as she pulled Nucci's arms behind him and began tying his wrists. "It's for him. You can get it from the toilet if you like. He'll be easier to move if he's awake."

Just then, Charity heard the uneven clip-clop of DJ's steps on the stairs. His stride was symmetrical, but the prosthetic made a slightly different sound. His footfalls on the boards were accompanied by the clicking of high heels.

"Let Blunt in," she told Layla, as she finished a series of tight loops and knots. "But check to make sure it's him. It sounds like someone's with him."

There was a tap on the door. "It's Blunt."

Layla opened the door, and he came in with the woman from the pictures. She seemed very hesitant, until she saw Nucci lying bound and unconscious on the couch.

Before anyone could move or say a word, the woman charged at the helpless man, grabbing up the wooden chair Charity had been sitting in.

Layla caught her around the waist before she could bring the chair crashing down on Nucci's skull. "Don't be like them, Jo!"

Them? Charity wondered.

The chair clattered to the floor as the woman turned and fell into her friend's embrace.

"Gabby," DJ said, turning to face her, "meet Joanne—Antoine Nucci's *fifth* victim."

CHAPTER THIRTY-TWO

Layla took Joanne into her bedroom to calm the woman as DJ related the story she'd told him about her conversations with Antoine Nucci, both before and after he'd drugged her.

She'd told DJ that he'd claimed to be a psychologist, specializing in divorce trauma, and he'd even given her a business card. Then he'd told her that her friend Layla had suggested he might be able to help her cope with the fallout from her divorce.

"She told me that she'd been a wreck when she'd left the lawyer at the café earlier today," DJ relayed. "Said she'd thought Providence was guiding her when he came along and they'd talked a little, as they walked together back toward her office, which was just past Nucci's house. Knowing the neighborhood, she didn't think it odd when he told her it was his office. A lot of the houses on that block are businesses. So, she'd agreed to stop and talk with him for a few minutes longer."

"How did he subdue her?" Charity asked, glancing toward the closed bedroom door.

"Slipped a Mickey in a glass of water," he replied. "Before she knew what was happening, he was forcing her down to the basement and she was helpless to fight back."

"You said she was his fifth victim?" Charity asked, pacing the floor next to Nucci's prone body.

"Yeah," he replied. "Um, is he dead?"

"No, I just knocked him out."

"Too bad," DJ said, looking down at the man as if he were going to spit on him.

"I might kill him yet," she said earnestly. "So, don't let bravado influence your words. I need to know if you're in or out."

"Seriously?" he said with genuine surprise. "You're going to murder him?"

"That's such a harsh word," Charity said.

DJ looked down at the unconscious man at his feet for a moment. "If half of what Joanne said is true," he finally muttered, looking up at her, "then he deserves it."

"What happened to the other four victims?"

It was DJ's turn to pace the floor. "He claimed to have abducted four other recently divorced women, using the same spiel." He stopped clip-clopping across the floor and looked at Charity with sad eyes. "Told her he'd kept them drugged up in his basement, degrading them into submission."

"He told her that?"

DJ nodded. "He even told her their names. She said he seemed to enjoy describing the process he'd used to break the others and she'd break just as easily."

"What else?"

DJ resumed pacing, as if he didn't want to look at her. "She said that he'd bragged how once he'd hooked them on oxycodone, he put them to work in his club, mostly in the back rooms, where patrons had sex with them for money."

"He told her all that?" Charity asked looking down at Nucci.

DJ waited until she looked back up at him.

"Yeah. And he also told Joanne that he'd killed them when they were used up and could no longer perform."

Layla came back into the room then. "She's resting," she said, then leaned on the kitchen table and sighed. "I can't believe I actually helped him."

"You shouldn't beat yourself up," DJ said. "You had no way of knowing."

"What are you going to do with him?"

"Do you have a printer?" DJ asked.

"Well, yeah. Why?"

"I asked Joanne if she'd testify if she had a day or two to recover," DJ told Charity. "We can print those pictures I took and write on them that she will come to the police station tomorrow to swear out a complaint of kidnapping and rape, and to report four murders. We can drop him off, all trussed up like a turkey, right outside the station using his car. That would be enough for them to hold him overnight, wouldn't it?"

Charity thought for a moment. Her first inclination would be to do just as Layla had suggested and drown him in the bay. But shoot him first to make sure he didn't come back. It wasn't like she hadn't done it before. But in those instances, she'd been sent to do it by her country, and it had never been on American soil.

"Okay," Charity finally agreed. "Print the pictures. If I were the desk sergeant, there's no way I'd let Nucci walk until detectives talked to her, whether she came in on her own or they went out and found her."

Five minutes later, Charity and DJ were ready to leave. She took the water Layla had brought and poured it over the side of Nucci's face. He sputtered and grunted when it got up his nose, then jerked awake, struggling to get away from the drenching.

"Sorry for the mess," Charity said, handing the glass to Layla.

Layla took it and put it on the table. "So, Jo won't have to go to the cops until tomorrow?"

"Or the next day," DJ said, reaching down with his good arm to grab the collar of Nucci's shirt and haul him up to his feet one-handed.

"Or the day after that," Charity said, as Joanne appeared at the bedroom door. "Or the day after that, or next week," she said to Joanne in an understanding tone. "When you're ready. But don't take too long. What I wrote on those pictures will keep him locked up until they find and talk to you. And they *will* come looking."

Joanne turned toward Nucci. His head was slumped and his hair matted his face. His right eye was already bruising and the eye bloodshot.

"I'll go in tomorrow," Joanne said. "And when he goes on trial, I'll give the jury the names he told me and how he'd bragged about what he'd done to those women. And I'll swear on a stack of Bibles what he did to me."

"He'll be put away for a long time," Charity assured her. "And if they can tie him to other women who've disappeared, he'll go to the electric chair." She looked back to where DJ held Nucci against the wall by the door. "Personally, I like Layla's idea. I'd even row him out into the bay myself."

"I have a boat," Joanne said, then stepped closer to Nucci and screamed, "I got it in my divorce, asshole! You didn't break me!"

Layla took her friend by the shoulders and steered her back toward the bedroom. Joanne stopped and turned around, looking at Charity for several seconds, searching her eyes. "This happened to you, didn't it?"

For a moment Charity's face softened as she looked from one woman to the other. She could see it in Layla's eyes too. She'd also been the victim of abuse. Slowly, she nodded her head once and recognized the look of compassion both women exhibited toward her.

"We better go," DJ said.

Instantly, Charity's features hardened as she glanced back. When she faced the two women again, she nodded more firmly. "You don't know us. You never saw us. Layla got you loose and you hit Nucci with a lamp and tied him up. Then Layla dropped him at the station using Nucci's car."

Layla nodded. "We'll come up with all the details before tomorrow."

Charity turned and opened the door for DJ, who forced Nucci through and started down the steps. He seemed to be able to walk okay and DJ had a firm grip on his shirt collar.

The night was quiet, save for a couple of night birds chirping away in the trees. They descended the steps, and when the trio reached the bottom, DJ marched the man straight toward his own car.

Charity knew there would be security cameras in front of the police station. But if DJ stayed low in the backseat, he could open the door and push Nucci out without being seen, and Charity could easily pull her blond hair over her face. The police would believe Layla later on when she told them it was her driving Nucci's car.

Suddenly, a gray sedan swerved into the exit, bouncing high over the sidewalk, then stopping at an angle behind Nucci's BMW. Two men with guns jumped out, and Charity recognized the man from the club.

With no time to think, Charity pulled her skirt up and grabbed her weapon as she moved to the left. There was a flurry of gunfire and then it was quiet.

Both men lay on the ground, unmoving.

When she looked over, DJ was standing with his left arm

extended, smoke curling from the Glock's suppressor.

She and DJ advanced on the two men, weapons at the ready. Each had a large red stain spreading across his chest. They were both obviously dead, blank eyes staring up at the night sky.

"I guess that solves the mystery," DJ said, turning back toward Nucci, still lying in the alley.

"What mystery?" Charity asked.

"Who's better?" he replied with a shrug, which caused him to wince from the pain it inflicted. "My guy hit the ground first."

Charity looked over to see him smiling.

"Yeah, he was the guy from the club," she said.

"So, we're in agreement?"

"Your guy's family jewels were the size of tennis balls. A sharp glance would've made him ball up."

"That don't have nothing to do with it."

"And he was short," she said. "Mine was taller. So, of course yours hit the ground first. But mine was dead first."

When they reached Nucci, he had *two* stains on his shirt, but the same empty look in his eyes. Charity glanced up and saw Layla and Joanne at the top of the steps, clutching one another.

"Cut his bindings," she ordered DJ, "and wipe his car down. It'll look like rival drug dealers and somebody got away. Is your Kimber registered?"

He glanced up with a smug, questioning look, then nodded toward the apartment. "Hurry. Someone's sure to have heard that."

But his words came out as Charity was already running up the steps.

She reached the landing and herded the two women inside. "We've had a slight hiccup in our plan."

CHAPTER THIRTY-THREE

Joanne's Ford Fusion was also parked in the one-way alley, but it was facing the right direction, unlike the other two cars. She and DJ had walked to her office, then driven to Layla's apartment in her car, parking by the café's drive-thru.

Charity got in the passenger side and DJ got in back so he could sit sideways.

"Are you sure you're okay with all this?" Charity asked the brunette when she started the engine.

She just stared through the windshield at the carnage in the alley—three men dead. Layla would wait until they drove away to call 911, but that didn't mean somebody else didn't call it in, so time was of the essence.

"We need to go," Charity said. "But I want to know for sure that you can live with what happened here tonight."

She put the car in gear and had to back up twice to turn around in the narrow alley, as the bodies and the dead men's car blocked the exit.

"I'm fine," she finally said, as she turned back out onto the street. "He got what he deserved."

"He did," Charity said, nodding slowly. "But the families of those other women won't have closure."

She drove in silence for a few blocks, then glanced quickly over at Charity, then to the backseat. "Layla and I were both sexually assaulted before this. Our exes couldn't process things and we each drifted apart from them."

Charity put a hand on hers, resting on the console. "It's not going to go away."

"When?" Joanne asked. "For you, I mean."

Charity glanced back at DJ, slumped in the backseat. His eyes were closed.

"Almost twenty years ago," she said quietly. "In Afghanistan. I was a helo pilot and got shot down and captured by the enemy."

Joanne looked over and locked eyes with Charity as the car sat idling at a traffic light. A tear formed in the corner of her left eye and rolled down her cheek. "I'm so sorry," she said. "It must have been nightmarish."

Still is, Charity thought, but said nothing.

"I never supported the war," Joanne said quietly. "I always thought people should settle their disputes with open dialogue."

Like many, Joanne Mitchell lived a life secluded from the horrors that existed daily in other parts of the world. Experiencing it twice hardly compared to what some people went through every day. But she was also shielded from it by the polite society she lived in. The long wars in the Middle East were just news stories to her and her friends—talking points.

"Nobody supports war," Charity said, turning and looking forward, her face bathed in the red glow of the traffic light. "And though I might disagree with things some people say about it, there will always be people like me" —she jerked a thumb toward the backseat— "and men like DJ back there, who will fight to the death to defend their right to say it."

"Is that where he lost his leg?" she asked.

"Iraq," Charity replied. "An IED explosion."

The light turned green, and Joanne looked in the mirror as she accelerated through the intersection. "You make a good couple, I think."

"We're not..." Charity began. "No. We just...we work together." She glanced quickly back at him again. "But he is kinda cute at times."

They drove in silence for a couple of miles. Finally, Joanne said, "I can still come forward against him."

"What do you mean?" Charity asked.

"When the news hits about the shooting, I can go to the police. I can say I was scared he'd come after me. Then I could tell them about the other girls."

Charity thought about it. Could she do it? It happened all the time. Several women had already come forward after Eisenstein's death, implicating other men with whom he was involved.

"You'd do that?" Charity asked. "There would be a public investigation."

She didn't answer right away, just drove for another half block as streetlights passed over the car, each one illuminating both their faces for a moment.

Then she nodded. "Yes, I'd do it. If only to let those families get the answers they deserve."

They turned off the road into the parking lot of the nightclub where Charity had left her car.

"Over there," Charity said, pointing. "The little blue convertible."

"The Miata?"

"It's actually a Fiat. Same frame and body, just a different engine and a more sedate and comfortable ride."

DJ sat up in the backseat when Joanne pulled into a parking spot next to Charity's car. "We're here?" he asked. "I musta dozed off."

"Yeah," Charity said. "And I don't blame you. I'm bushed."

Joanne got out of the car, then gently hugged DJ, kissing him on the cheek. "I never got a chance to thank you," she said. "You saved my life."

Even under the dim glow of the orange lights scattered around the parking lot, Charity could see his face flush, and she grinned.

"Anyone woulda done it," he said. "Your knight in shining armor is nothing more than a one-legged, one-armed pirate."

Joanne laughed. "All you need is an eyepatch and a parrot."

Charity thought it was great to hear her laughing, considering what she'd been through. There might be nights in her future when she would relive her experience.

The two women hugged, and Joanne said, "Thank you for everything, and if you ever need someone, I'm here. Layla too."

They said their final goodbyes and Charity took her trauma kit from the backseat and put it in the Fiat's trunk. Joanne was driving away when Charity got in and started the engine

DJ folded himself into the passenger seat. "Want to drive straight back?" he asked. "That was a quick day's work."

"A long one, though," Charity replied. "Let's go back to the hotel. I don't feel like driving until I can get some sleep."

She caught his lewd grin as he said, "I'm all for that."

"Two beds, Deej," she said. "Tomorrow's going to be a long day, too. I still have to report to Mr. Conti."

"Can't blame a guy for tryin'," he said, still grinning. But this time it was more like the banter of a fun-loving friend. Then his expression became serious. "I'll go with you to see the boy's family if you want."

"I could probably use the support," she said. "But you don't—"

"I want to," he said, turning his attention to his phone's mapping software to get them back to the hotel. He pointed at Joanne's Ford leaving the parking lot. "Same way she's going. Two miles, then a left."

They drove on in comparative silence, DJ only speaking to give Charity directions and distances to the next turn. They were both beyond just being tired. Their day had started at first light, with her pointing a gun at him, and the adrenaline peaks throughout the day had taken their toll. Charity's thoughts were on what happened earlier and what she might have done differently to reduce the bloodshed. She had no idea who the second gunman was who'd showed up with Boudreaux's hitman. An associate? Backup? Somebody he'd hired in the bar? Whatever, his agreeing to go had brought about his death.

Finally, they arrived back at the hotel. Charity parked the car and shut off the engine, having decided there was nothing short of killing the man at the club that would have changed anything.

DJ turned to face her. "Did we do the right thing here tonight?" he asked.

Charity just stared through the windshield. Her mind had been skewed by past missions and assignments and she sometimes wasn't all that sure where the lines were anymore.

"I mean, we were going to do what's right," he said.

Charity knew he was only arguing with himself and let him get it all out.

"So, we were doing it a little underhanded," he said, trying to justify what they'd done. "Even selfish, I guess, because it left everything on those two girls. Then it got out of our control, right?"

243

Charity turned slowly, looking at DJ in the low glow of landscape lights. "Legally?" she began, speaking softly. "We'd be arrested and charged with murder. I don't think we left anything in the form of physical evidence at all, except the two slugs, and neither is traceable to us. I *would* suggest ditching our guns at the first available chance—somewhere deep. But if they find anything else, we'd be facing at least twenty years. Morally? Those two men came looking to kill Nucci and they were spoiling for a fight. They got one." She paused. "It never bothers me when someone who is trying to kill me ends up dead. What you have to wrestle with is whether you can accept being a man of good moral standing *while* you are violating the law. In the eyes of the courts, we are murderers. But in *my* eyes, we saved the taxpayers a lot of money. I'm okay with it coming down to just that."

He only stared at her for a moment.

"What?" she asked. "Do I have something on me?"

He grinned. "I don't think I've ever heard you say more than a few words at one time."

When they got to the room, DJ pointed toward the bathroom. "Let me take a leak and it's all yours. I'll shower in the morning. Right now, I just want to sleep."

When he came out, Charity took a quick shower and pulled on the clothes she was going to wear to drive back to Apalachicola. Then she padded quietly back into the room in bare feet.

DJ was asleep on top of the covers, the edge of the bedspread tossed up over his missing limb, as if he didn't want her to see it, even as he slept. His prosthetic lay on the floor beside the bed, mute testament to what the man had been through. Charity stared at it for a moment, then looked up at DJ's face.

For an instant, she felt fortunate.

ELUSIVE CHARITY

They both carried the psychological and emotional scars of war. She knew enough about the man's background to understand that he'd been through Hell more than once.

On occasion, Charity's own psychological wounds would disappear and she could laugh and behave like a normal person. Those instances didn't come often, but they did happen.

DJ was reminded of his torment every minute of every day. And on top of that, his foot—cremated, incinerated, and dumped in a landfill thousands of miles away—still itched.

She stuffed her dirty clothes into her bag and stretched out on the other bed, staring up at the ceiling while she listened to DJ's deep breathing. Then she closed her eyes and was soon asleep.

CHAPTER THIRTY-FOUR

Behind closed lids, Charity's eyes darted back and forth in desperation. She clenched them tightly in her sleep and moaned as she slid into the dream, succumbing to what was inevitable as blackness swirled around her.

Suddenly, she was in the pilot's seat, struggling with the controls, trying to slow the aircraft's violent spin toward the ground. The tail rotor was out and the Huey's turbine was redlining as she attempted to maintain partial control. The crash was imminent; it was just a matter of how hard they'd hit the ground.

Her copilot was dead, slumped in his harness, half his face blown away by shrapnel. Half a dozen wounded soldiers were in the back. They'd been evacuated from just outside Kandahar.

The rugged terrain came up toward her at an alarming rate. At the last second, she pulled up hard on the collective, then shut off the fuel flow to the turbine. For that one second, the bird almost stopped its crazy spin just before hitting the ground and somersaulting forward and to the right.

Charity heard the terrible crunching sound as the skids and then the airframe collapsed in slow motion. The sound of the rotors striking the earth were like machine-gun fire and she saw the huge plumes of sand they kicked up before the blades failed and broke into shards, flying in every direction.

She felt the violent impact through her harness straps, which strained to hold her in place as her body was still moving forward at seventy knots. They wrenched her shoulders, digging into her collarbones, while the lap belt's pressure gave the sensation of expelling her stomach and intestines from her body.

There was no explosion, *she realized, as she quickly removed her flight helmet and began struggling to get out of the harness. Every movement hurt, but she had to get out of the aircraft.*

There wasn't anything she could do for Lieutenant Fields in the left seat, but if any of the men in back were still alive, she'd also have to get them out.

A thundering of hooves approached, and before she could get free, a Taliban fighter jumped from his horse and stood before her, raising a rifle.

"Laa!" a large man with a scar on his face shouted. "Hadhih aimra'a!"

He wasn't speaking Pashto, as most of the people of the region did. It was Arabic and he'd told the man not to shoot her because she was a woman.

The horses spooked and shied and one reared, nearly dumping its rider, afraid of the ticking time bomb that was her helicopter.

The scar-faced man shouted at the others, giving orders to kill all but the woman. Charity turned in her seat and looked on in horror as several horsemen opened fire on the injured and helpless men in her charge.

She barely stifled a scream...

On the next bed, DJ's right leg moved, stretching and flexing, rubbing the stump of his lower leg against the rough bed covering. He didn't awaken, but a low, mournful moan escaped his lips as he, too, slid into the same nightmare he'd had countless nights for nearly twenty years.

ELUSIVE CHARITY

He was on the outskirts of Fallujah, where only sporadic fighting had erupted for several days. A few of the more seasoned soldiers sensed something looming on the horizon.

Two squads moved along opposite sides of the street. They were members of Company B—the "Renegades"—of the 2nd Battalion, 502nd Infantry Regiment, of the famed 101st Airborne Division.

"Five-O-Deuce," as the regiment was called, as well as other elements of the 101st "Screaming Eagle" Division, had just replaced 82nd Airborne as part of the security force maintaining peace since the overthrow of Saddam Hussein's Ba'ath Party. The hunt for the ousted leader was in its fourth month, though it had only taken five weeks to overwhelm Iraqi forces and take the capital.

"Roger that," Specialist Guthrie said into his handset, before turning to DJ. "Vehicles are inbound for pickup, Sergeant Martin."

The sound of the big HMMWV's tires crunching across broken stone could be heard approaching from the south. The Humvee, as it had come to be known, was a nimble little truck, equally at home on city streets as it was in the desert sand.

Three of them rounded a corner and approached the block where DJ and his squad were hunkered down, on high alert. There wasn't much worry; fighting had all but stopped throughout the country. But it always paid to stay on guard.

Just as the first Humvee came to a stop, DJ heard a whooshing sound, which he recognized instantly.

Suddenly, before anyone could shout a word of warning, the lead vehicle went up in a giant fireball, lifting completely off the ground. The massive explosion flipped the Humvee backward, almost landing on the second vehicle. A rocket-propelled grenade had shattered the windshield, exploding inside the vehicle, and killing the driver instantly.

DJ's squad returned fire, as did Sergeant Blount's men on the other side

249

of the street.

More RPGs and small arms fire rained down from the high rooftops as the enemy tried to wipe out both squads.

Guthrie was already calling in for air support, anticipating DJ's orders.

"Get those trucks out of here!" DJ shouted.

In their excitement after the first accurate rocket hit, the enemy fighters hadn't been able to aim subsequent rockets as precisely, and the two remaining Humvees backed up the street at high speed.

Being on the ground and having enemy fighters shooting down from above was an untenable situation. Across the street, Sergeant Blount could also see that, and was ordering his men back.

"Fall back!" DJ shouted, firing steadily as the men ahead of him dropped back to take positions of cover.

Finally, DJ and Guthrie rose and sprinted toward the rear as the rest of their squad opened up on the rooftops.

They ducked behind a large piece of concrete that had fallen from the top of a building, taking cover, and returning fire once more as the squad leap-frogged past them.

Moving his right foot to get into a better shooting position, DJ felt something give beneath his boot.

There was a metallic click.

His eyes went wide with terror.

Time slowed.

DJ turned to shout a warning to Guthrie, but his radioman was already moving, having also heard the unmistakable sound of the IED's trigger mechanism.

As DJ attempted to jump and push Guthrie out of the way, the younger soldier leapt over him.

The IED exploded, sending both men cartwheeling into the street.

As quickly as it had started, the shooting stopped, and Charity saw the faces of the dead men in the back of her broken aircraft. In an instant, each one was indelibly stamped in her memory. Each one someone's son, brother, father, cousin, or friend. Each one struck down in the prime of life, forever ending what might come after.

The man who'd been pointing his rifle at her smashed out what remained of the windshield, reached in, and grabbed Charity by the hair, pulling her through the jagged opening.

The scar-faced man brought his horse up next to them, reached down and grabbed the collar of Charity's flight suit, yanking her up onto his horse. She was draped unceremoniously across his thighs and the horse's neck.

Yelling and screaming with bloodlust, the horsemen rode off, expertly dodging around boulders and threading their way down into the valley.

On the edge of waking, Charity knew they were going back to the torture cave. She also knew the nightmare wouldn't release her. Not just yet. More pain was coming.

The horsemen continued down the boulder-strewn mountainside, crossed a dry stream bed, then started up the other side. They weren't going nearly as fast now, the horses laboring.

Charity struggled, trying to throw herself off the horse. But the man clubbed her in the back of the head with a heavy fist, and everything went black.

The pain in his leg was excruciating, yet DJ managed to drag Guthrie's body down into the crater the IED had created. The man was dead; of that, there wasn't any doubt. What DJ had dragged was nothing more than the man's torso, with one leg barely attached. The radio was equally as dead.

Suddenly, Sergeant Blount was beside him. "I got you, buddy," he said, *dragging DJ farther into the crater as the sound of helicopters approached.*

The other sergeant quickly put a tourniquet around DJ's leg just below his knee, making it tighter and tighter as DJ grimaced in pain.

"I saw what happened," Sergeant Blount said, grabbing DJ and pulling him upright until he was sitting with his back against the bigger man's chest. DJ looked down, and where his right foot had once been, nothing remained except a bloody stump with the shards of his shin sticking out.

"I saw what your radioman did," Blount said again. "He saved your life, man!"

An Iraqi fighter came rushing around the corner, shooting wildly.

Blount raised his rifle and squeezed off a burst, stitching the man from his crotch to his shoulder.

"I got your six, buddy," Blount moaned.

An anguished, guttural scream woke Charity, just as the horsemen in her recurring nightmare reached the entrance to the cave where she'd been tortured and brutalized. The loud cry, coupled with the nightmarish revisitation, elicited a scream of her own as she lunged for safety between the two beds.

She and DJ collided and fell to the floor, both grabbing at one another in sheer terror. They embraced and rolled on the floor, each holding the other's head close to their shoulders in panic, protection, desperation, and empathy.

CHAPTER THIRTY-FIVE

It was close to noon when Charity guided her little sports car to a stop at the marina where she'd picked up DJ the day before. Jojo's black BMW was sitting there, but she didn't see him.

Suddenly the driver's door opened, and Jojo climbed out.

"Who's that?" DJ asked, seeing her expression.

They hadn't talked much during the drive back to Apalachicola that morning. They got a late start because they'd stayed up most of the night talking, after being thrust together by the recurrent nightmares they'd both endured for years. They'd found that in the darkness, they could talk to one another freely.

Charity had opened up to the man, just a little at first, while they'd lain on the floor. They'd both been breathing hard and sweating, so it had been obvious to both what had happened.

At first, they'd laughed. Uproarious laughter at where they'd found themselves. Then they stopped, each remembering what had brought them there.

DJ had told her about Phil Guthrie, his radioman in Iraq, and how he'd given his life for DJ. Then he'd told her about his friend, Sergeant Bobby Blount, who'd been shot and wounded while trying to save him, and how he'd ended up being hanged by police officers in Puerto Rico ten years later.

Charity had in turn told DJ about the men in the back of her helicopter, and how they'd all been shot to death, except Zach Barkley, who they'd both met briefly aboard *Ambrosia*, the day they'd all signed on to work for Armstrong. Before the night was over, she'd told him about the repeated rape and the great satisfaction she'd felt when she'd spilled the scar-faced man's blood.

They'd finally fallen asleep next to one another on Charity's bed, fully clothed, each holding and protecting the other.

"I told you about him," Charity replied. "His name's Jojo—the guy I first suspected."

"Rightly so," DJ said. "He fits the description to a T."

They got out and Jojo approached, smiling warmly.

"Namaste, Charity," he said, placing his palms together. "I was just wondering if I'd see you again before we left, and here you are."

"Jojo, I'd like you to meet an associate of mine, DJ Martin," Charity said. "DJ, this is Jyotiraditya Laghari, but everyone just calls him Jojo."

He gave Charity a surprised look as he shook DJ's offered left hand.

"You even got the inflection correct. I'm flattered." Then he turned to DJ and nodded toward the sling. "You're injured?"

"Just a scratch," DJ said.

"I trust that the pain is not too great," Jojo offered.

"I'll survive it."

"DJ, is it?" Jojo asked. "Don Johnson? Davey Jones?"

DJ laughed. "I'll take a cop and the keeper of the deep for one thousand, Alex. But I guess it's Ken now, or Blossom, or Amy, or whatever *her* name is."

Charity held back a snicker at Jojo's obvious puzzlement. "So, what brings you here?" he asked.

"The *Whole Nine Yards*," DJ replied.

Jojo's face brightened. "Ah, the beautiful twenty-seven-footer docked in front of me. Clever name."

"We bumped into each other early yesterday morning," Charity explained. "I wasn't even aware DJ was in the area."

"I'm pleased that I found you," Jojo said. "I'm hosting a small farewell gathering for The Buddha at the Haverstocks' this evening at sunset. Just some close friends and followers. It would bring us great pleasure if you would both join us."

"I don't—" Charity began.

"Please accept," Jojo said, then smiled warmly. "The Buddha will only lure you out of hiding with his bowls."

"Sure," DJ said. "But we'll have to make it an early night. I'm flying to Bimini in the morning, myself, and Charity has offered to take me to the airport."

Charity turned and looked at him, surprised.

"You convinced me last night," he said.

"Then I won't keep you," Jojo said. "I only stopped by to secure my boat."

Jojo turned and got back into his car as Charity and DJ walked down the dock.

"Are you sure about going back?" Charity asked.

"I still have a debt to pay," DJ replied. "Last night was a reminder."

"Then I'll be happy to take you to the airport," she said. "But you don't have to go to this thing at the Haverstocks' tonight. Jojo and The Buddha are a pair of Hindu spiritualists from Bangladesh. I'm sure you'll find it very boring."

"I don't think hanging around you would ever get boring," he replied, stepping aboard his boat.

"Okay, but don't say I didn't warn you," she said. "Want me to pick you up here? Say, about seven?"

He nodded toward the little eight-foot dinghy tied off to the stern. "I can meet you there. Where is it?"

She gave him the location of where her boat was just east of the airstrip and that she was anchored behind the Haverstocks' house, then they said goodbye, and she started walking back to her car.

"You didn't say what to wear," he called after her.

She tossed her hair over her shoulder and looked back. "Island casual, of course."

On the drive back over the two long bridges, she thought again about the previous night and wondered if Joanne had gone to the police yet. She couldn't fault her if she'd backed out. She was safe but making her story public would be even more humiliating.

She thought again about her long discussion with DJ as the two lay beside each other on the floor, then later on her bed. After a few moments, noticing the chop on the bay, she became concerned about how DJ would manage the waves in his little tender. With a missing leg and an arm in a sling, it could be dangerous.

Then she remembered something he'd said. About how he felt there was some power beyond their comprehension that had put Guthrie and Blount with him that day and how he knew he wasn't finished yet because he hadn't yet earned their lives. He'd said he knew that whatever controlled everything had plans for him, and that thought would always get him through hardships.

"The world better watch out for DJ Martin," she said aloud, her words disappearing with the wind.

CHAPTER THIRTY-SIX

It was still half an hour before sunset when Charity shut off the outboard on her dinghy and tied the painter off to the Haverstocks' dock. She'd waited as long as she could, but DJ hadn't arrived at her boat and there was no other dinghy tied up to the pier. She'd had doubts about whether or not he'd come. That was probably why he'd insisted on her not picking him up.

As she made her way toward the foot of the pier, she stopped halfway and observed the people milling about on the deck. Then, from out over the water, a faint buzzing sound caught her attention.

She looked back and could just make out a small boat heading toward her in the gathering dusk. After a moment, as it got closer, she recognized DJ at the tiller and walked back out to the covered dock to meet him.

"Hiya, Charity," he said, as he brought his little boat alongside the dock. "Sorry I'm late. Couldn't find a thing to wear."

He killed the engine and when he drifted close enough, flung a dock line toward her with his left hand. His right lay on the side of the boat, and he wasn't wearing a sling.

"How's the shoulder?" she asked, stomping on the line before picking it up and tying it off to a deck cleat.

"Still burns like all hell," he replied, climbing awkwardly up the ladder. "But as long as I don't move it much, I think it'll be okay. Still, changing the back bandage was a bit tricky."

"I'm so sorry," Charity said. "I should've—"

"Don't worry about it," he said. "I figured out a way."

The two strolled along the dock toward the house, where Charity could now hear the sound of The Buddha's bowls.

"What in the heck is that?" DJ asked.

"Singing bowls," Charity replied, noticing a young woman lying on a blanket next to The Buddha, her hands clasped over her belly. "I have one beside my bed on the boat. The Buddha gave it to me."

"What's he doing?"

"I don't know," Charity said, as they reached shore and started across the lawn.

Jojo separated himself from the others and approached them.

"Namaste," he said, pressing his palms together. "I'm so happy you both came." He glanced down at DJ's legs, exposed below the cargo shorts he wore, as DJ absently rubbed the back of the shoe against his good leg. Then he looked him in the eye. "I see you're no longer wearing the sling. Your arm is better?"

"A little," DJ replied.

"You are next, then."

"Next what?" DJ asked uncomfortably.

Jojo turned and waved a hand toward where The Buddha sat on a mat, cross-legged and with his eyes closed, as he made eerie sounds and bongs using several bowls arranged around him.

"We are doing sound healings," Jojo said. "The Buddha can help with your healing."

"Oh, I don't—" DJ began, lifting his right leg, and wincing when he tried to reach down with his injured arm to scratch an itch that wasn't there.

"I don't mean your shoulder, my friend," Jojo said, noticing DJ's frustration. "Sound healing is for the spirit and the mind. It may make the pain in your shoulder more tolerable, but it will not miraculously heal your physical wounds. You are not ignorant. The pain or discomfort you feel in your foot isn't real. It is only a manifestation in your mind."

"And this Buddha guy can fix that?"

Jojo smiled. "*The* Buddha," he replied. "His real name is Daljeet Khatri and he is a true spiritual healer."

"So, what's wrong with the girl?" DJ asked, jutting his chin in that direction.

"Like you, her pain is in her mind. Gail is a recovering addict."

Charity looked over at the woman lying on The Buddha's mat. She was dressed nicely, had long, lustrous, blond hair, looked to be very fit, and to all outward appearance, was the picture of health. Not the stereotype of an addict at all. She lay with her head on a pillow and a dark blue stone on her forehead. Another, that looked like a large emerald, sat on her sternum.

"The indigo stone represents the third eye—the sixth chakra," Jojo explained quietly. "The third eye is what provides us intuition and awareness. It manifests itself in one's charisma. The green stone on her chest is the fourth chakra—the heart—which allows us to love and give compassion toward others. Gail has been clean and sober for five years and now runs an intervention group to help others recover from addiction. The Buddha is primarily playing the bowls that emit the E and C tones, also associated with those chakras."

"What was the bowl he gave me?" Charity asked, suddenly more interested.

"The fourth chakra," he replied, taking her hand, and pressing a small green stone into it. "The heart chakra. The tone is C for the very elusive Charity."

She smiled and looked down at the stone.

The Buddha stopped his bowls, then leaned over and removed the two stones from the young woman as her eyes blinked and fluttered open.

"Come," Jojo said, motioning them forward.

"I'm not real sure about any of this," DJ said apprehensively.

"You're not afraid, are you?" Charity chided. "Just do it, DJ. I did it a couple of days ago and it was very relaxing."

As the woman got to her feet, The Buddha looked toward them and smiled. "Ah, Miss Charity," he said, eyes sparkling. "And you have brought a friend."

Jojo put his palms together and nodded his head slightly. "This is DJ Martin," he told The Buddha. "He has recently injured his arm and suffers from a long-ago leg injury."

The Buddha glanced down at DJ's fake leg, then swept a hand toward the mat Gail had just vacated. She now stood with a handsome young man, both smiling as if they'd just received the best news in the world.

"Please sit down, DJ," The Buddha said. "And if you wouldn't mind, please remove your shirt."

DJ's eyes darted to Charity in alarm. Without knowing why, she simply nodded her head, and he started unsnapping his shirt. Several people gasped slightly when the front and back bandages were revealed.

"Tell me about your leg," The Buddha said, ignoring the bandages.

"It's not there." DJ said.

The Buddha smiled, mischievously. "Where is it?"

"In some landfill in Iraq," DJ bluntly replied.

"That's good," The Buddha said. "We have established that it is no longer attached to your body and therefore cannot cause you pain."

"It's more of an itch," DJ volunteered.

"An itch that is obviously in your mind," The Buddha said. "Now, lie back on your mat as Gail was a moment ago. Make yourself as comfortable as you can and close your eyes. Don't try to concentrate on what you will hear, just hear it, and let the sounds carry you."

As DJ did so, propping his head on the thick pillow, The Buddha chose a deep violet stone and placed it on the crown of his head. Then he took an orange stone and placed it low on his belly, right at his belt.

"I didn't expect to see you here," a man's voice said.

Charity turned to find Angelo and Gina Conti standing beside her.

"Mr. Conti," Charity said. "I was planning to come and see you in the morning."

"You are a devotee of The Buddha?" Gina asked.

"Devo—, um no, I'm a friend of Rudy and Heather, the couple who lives here. That's my boat out there on the bay."

The bowls started singing. The tones were different than those The Buddha had used with the young woman.

"Your friend seems anguished," Angelo said. "His injury. Was he shot recently?"

Charity glanced over at DJ, resting comfortably on the mat. "Yes, he was. He got shot protecting the man who sold the drugs that killed Jeff Pender and Karin Bishop."

"Protecting him?"

"It was early in our investigation," Charity said, then turned to face the couple. "Later, when we had evidence and were getting ready to take the drug dealer to the police, the man who tried to kill him the first time came back for another try."

"Is he...?" Gina Conti started to ask.

"Very dead," Charity replied. "His name was Antoine Nucci and his career as a criminal is over."

"And you're sure he was the man who sold Jeff the drugs?"

"Either directly or indirectly," Charity replied, seeing no need in telling the couple about Nucci's other crimes. "Yes, I'm sure."

"I see," Angelo said, then turned to watch The Buddha. "The seventh chakra is the crown," Angelo explained quietly, almost reverently. "It represents understanding, wisdom, and spirituality. The orange stone is the sacral chakra, having to do with feelings, emotions, and sexuality."

"I understand the crown part," Charity said. "My friend has a phantom itch in his missing right foot. But what's that got to do with sex?"

Gina smiled. "Not just sex. Our sexuality is one of the strongest driving forces of our spirit. When the sacral chakra is in harmony, it affects the whole body's feeling of well-being."

The Contis went back to their friends, leaving Charity alone. After several more minutes, the bowls stopped, and DJ sat up. He and The Buddha exchanged a few words, then DJ got to his feet and came toward her, putting his shirt back on.

"How do you feel?" she asked.

"Weird," he replied. "For a second, I felt like I was floating in warm water. Then he said something, and I sat up. Don't know what a couple of bings and bongs can do."

She smiled up at him as he fastened the snaps on his shirt. "You were lying there for a good ten or twelve minutes."

"Ten—no way. It was just a couple of seconds."

The Contis started back toward them.

"Here comes Mr. Conti," she said. "I already told them all about what happened."

"When?"

She smiled up at him. "During those few seconds you were floating around in the water."

"I understand you were injured while investigating Jeff's death," Angelo said. "I'm deeply sorry for that. How does it feel now?"

"DJ, this is Angelo and Gina Conti," Charity said. "Mr. Conti, DJ Martin."

DJ shrugged slightly, then looked back at The Buddha, who had another person sitting on the mat talking to him. He turned and grinned at Charity. "It still hurts, but the burning feels more like a warm glow, if that makes any sense."

Angelo turned to his wife, who took an envelope from her purse and handed it to him.

"This is for you," he said, extending the envelope to DJ. "Rudy was kind enough to cash a check for us." DJ tried to wave the lawyer off but Conti was insistent. "For the pain this investigation has caused you."

DJ politely took the envelope and stuck it in his pocket. "Thanks."

"We must be leaving," Gina said. "We're driving home in the morning, now that Angelo can give Al and Dot some answers."

They shook hands again and Charity glanced down after they'd left and asked, "What did he give you?"

DJ pulled the envelope out and opened it, looking inside. Then he looked at Charity. "Didn't they already pay you?"

She nodded. "A five thousand-dollar retainer."

He opened the envelope and tilted it toward her. Charity saw it was stuffed with hundred-dollar bills.

"There's at least another five thousand in here," DJ said in disbelief.

"Oooh," Charity said, going for a seductive sound. "Muscles and money."

DJ smiled lewdly. "I don't need the man's money," he said.

"I know," Charity whispered, taking his good arm. "You wouldn't be working for Armstrong if you did."

She leaned away from the group, gently pulling on DJ's arm. He allowed her to drag him along, but discreetly dropped the envelope into one of The Buddha's bowls as they walked toward the pier.

"Where are we going?" he asked.

"I want to apologize for my harshness earlier," she said, smiling.

"What? When you said I should 'sail on' when this was over?"

She continued to pull him toward the long pier. "I want to show you my boat."

THE END

Afterword

Elusive Charity was a lot more fun to write than the earlier books in this series. I was able to dig a little deeper into what makes Charity tick, and by pairing her with DJ Martin, who Charity had had a bit of a spark with at the end of *Lost Charity*, I was able to peel back the layers with him as well.

Placing them both in Apalach was a no-brainer. If you remember, at the end of *Lost Charity*, she set sail for the Forgotten Coast. My good friend and colleague, Dawn Lee McKenna, had passed away just as I was finishing *Lost Charity* and I knew then what I wanted to do. So, I sent Charity on her way to the Forgotten Coast.

Dawn and I had talked often about swapping characters, as I've done with a few other writers, but we just never seriously got around to it, aside from me being a character in her first novel in the *Forgotten Coast Series* and she appearing as a Key West fortune teller in my *Fallen Honor*. So, with her mother and daughter's permission, I brought Maggie, Wyatt, and Boudreaux back for another bow. Sort of a "nod to the storyteller." If you haven't already read Dawn's books, start with *Low Tide* after this. You'll thank me later, when you come up to take your first breath of air in a few days after binge reading the whole series.

This may or may not be the last we'll see of Dawn's characters. I can't say anything more on that just yet, but "something sinister is afoot in Apalach."

As I write this afterword, I've barely got my land legs back after a week-long cruise through the British Virgin Islands and the Eastern Caribbean aboard a 400-foot-long four-masted schooner called *Star Flyer*.

Congratulations to Doug and Lynne Stebbins, who were on the cruise with us. Doug and Lynne were chosen from the group to be characters in *Cast Off*, which will be released in early November. Their characters will be themselves, with a bit of a fictional twist. We had eleven people in our little group; the cruise and company were terrific fun and something I'll remember always.

The last stop on our cruise was St. Bart's, which I'd never been to before. I wish we could have stayed there a week or two. I intend for it to be part of the setting for *Cast Off*.

If you don't mind a little salt spray, some rocking and rolling, and plenty of wind, I highly recommend Star Clippers Cruise Line, and particularly, *Star Flyer*. I was able to climb the rigging, hoist sails, and be on the bridge while underway. My daughter Jordan even got to pilot the ship for ten minutes.

However, I vehemently recommend you avoid American Airlines and Miami International Airport. We flew out of nearby Savannah, but next time, I'll drive two hundred miles to a hub in Atlanta or Charlotte for a direct flight. More on this nightmare when Jesse flies commercial in *Cast Off*. Y'all, everything's fodder for fiction. You don't think I came up with that transvesselite term several books back all by myself did you?

Today is Friday, March 25, and this book will be released in a little over five weeks. I greatly appreciate the many readers who have preordered this one, as well as all my other books. It's been nearly nine years since I started on my first book and this will be my thirtieth novel. Without you, my readers, this journey would never have gotten this far. I am continually in your grace.

Many thanks to Marsha Zinberg for the demanding work in editing this writer's butchery of the printed language. She's efficient, accurate, and I'm indebted to her for helping me write better.

By Monday, this manuscript will proceed to the next stage in editing, the final proofread, for whom I depend on Donna Rich. She's had the last critical eye on nearly all of my books.

As usual, this manuscript won't get to my audiobook narrator, Nick Sullivan, until it shines like a diamond. But Nick always finds a few things that might read better if changed slightly. So, I always wait until he finishes recording before sending the very last draft to Aurora Publicity for final formatting and uploading.

But before anyone reads any of my stories, the manuscript first goes to a team of close friends and professionals to check for accuracy and to look for holes I may have left in the plot, which happens a lot.

It takes me several months to come up with the story, and many members of my team will read the whole thing in a single day. So, there are often little plot devices or red herrings that I just forget to flesh out.

Many thanks to John Trainer, Debbie Kocol, Jason Hebert, Mike Ramsey, Drew Mutch, Charles Höfbauer, Dana Vihlen, Rick Iossi, Alan Fader, Glenn Hibbert, Katy McKnight, Thomas Crisp, and Kim DeWitt. Without your input, this story wouldn't be nearly as good.

As always, I thank God for his patience with me and for putting Greta in my life. My wife is the mortar that holds all the building blocks together. She's my anchor and rode, holding me fast. Our daughter Jordan is taking on more and more responsibility these days, running the online Ship's Store, maintaining inventory, reminding me of pending deadlines, and being an all around Girl Friday. One day soon, she'll take over everything while me and her mom travel. And for that, we're both thankful.

Thanks also to our other kids, Nikki, Laura, and Richard, as well as the extended family and grandkids, for all the support they continue to provide.

Lastly, a big thank you to my team at Down Island Press, Down Island Publishing, and Aurora Publicity. The support these people provide really makes my job as a storyteller a lot easier.

If you'd like to receive my newsletter, please sign up on my website.

WWW.WAYNESTINNETT.COM.

Once a month, I'll bring you insights into my private life and writing habits, with updates on what I'm working on, special deals I hear about, and new books by other authors that I'm reading.

The Jerry Snyder Caribbean Mystery Series

Wayward Sons

The Charity Styles Caribbean Thriller Series

Merciless Charity
Ruthless Charity
Reckless Charity
Elusive Charity
Enduring Charity
Vigilant Charity
Lost Charity

The Jesse McDermitt Caribbean Adventure Series

Fallen Out
Fallen Palm
Fallen Hunter
Fallen Pride
Fallen Mangrove
Fallen King
Fallen Honor
Fallen Tide
Fallen Angel
Fallen Hero
Rising Storm
Rising Fury
Rising Force
Rising Charity
Rising Water
Rising Spirit
Rising Thunder
Rising Warrior
Rising Moon
Rising Tide
Steady As She Goes
All Ahead Full
Man Overboard
Cast Off

The Gaspar's Revenge Ship's Store is open.

There, you can purchase all kinds of swag related to my books. You can find it at

WWW.GASPARS-REVENGE.COM

Made in the USA
Las Vegas, NV
14 February 2024

85813034R00154